This

Henry Humming®

1st Edition belongs to

_____

THE VICEROY PRESS

Henry Humming®  *Henry Saves Hanna*

By Irene Star

Illustrated by Eric Zeringue

THE VICEROY PRESS • LAPLACE, LA

© 2017 THE VICEROY PRESS • HENRY HUMMING is a registered trademark, Printed in USA.

ISBN 978-0-9993265-0-3   First Edition 2017

HENRY HUMMING

CHAPTER ONE

Henry and Hanna

A nest no bigger than half a ping-pong ball, made of twigs, feathers, and spider silk, rested on a slender branch of a crepe myrtle. It was decorated with paint chips taken from a whimsically painted fence. Bonnie Humming, the mama hummingbird, and Bob Humming, the papa hummingbird, had built this nest to start their family. Mama fluttered away in search of food, leaving two white eggs, no bigger than jellybeans, side by side in the nest.

One hummingbird egg began to hatch. Mama and Papa flew back just in time to watch. A tiny, featherless bird poked his head out. Though his eyes were closed, he managed a smile, which brought Mama and Papa great joy.

"Our little baby boy!" Mama sang.

"Let's call him Henry. Henry Humming," Papa hummed.

Mama and Papa turned their heads toward the other egg, but there was no change, no crack. And so they waited.

The next day, a small crack appeared on the tiny egg. Papa, Mama, and Henry watched the egg with excitement. Another crack appeared! *Crack, crack, crack!* Out popped a small featherless head. Her eyes were closed, and she wore a clumsy smile.

"Our little baby girl!" Mama sang.

"Let's call her Hanna. Hanna Humming," Papa hummed.

Hanna broke free from the rest of her egg. Papa and Mama stared in shock: Hanna only had one wing! Mama worried that she hadn't tended to Hanna's egg properly. Papa worried about Hanna's future as a bird. "Would she ever fly on her own?" Papa wondered. Henry, oblivious to anything amiss, nestled against his sister's neck lovingly.

Three weeks after hatching, on a particularly humid morning, Henry and Hanna lay side by side. The nest now bigger, as it stretched to accommodate Henry and Hanna's growth. The siblings looked more like real hummingbirds now that they had feathers. Their bills were long, straight, and very slender. Mama no longer had to feed them every twenty minutes.

Henry stretched, fluttered his wings, and flew a few inches out of the nest. Hanna watched in awe. Henry flew to the edge of the nest while Hanna sipped sweet nectar from a trumpet vine.

Proudly, Henry flew around the vine. When he landed back in the nest, Hanna nestled into her brother's neck as though to say, *"Please don't leave me behind."*

Papa and Mama returned to the nest with food.

"Papa, Mama, I flew! I flew all on my own," Henry said.

"That's wonderful, Henry!" Mama replied.

After hearing the praise for her brother, Hanna tried her best to fly as well. She flapped her one wing as hard as she could. She lifted herself a wee bit out of the nest before falling back inside. Hanna bashfully resumed her spot in the nest after failing to fly.

Papa and Mama realized they had to move their family to a stocked backyard. A backyard where they could live a long, safe life and be provided for by humans with bird feeders. Papa crouched down and Hanna climbed onto his back. Mama nodded toward Henry and they headed off to find the perfect home.

The first backyard was small but had a pretty garden of tulips and trumpet vines. An empty nest rested upon a thick branch of an oak tree. The Humming family landed in the nest only to be scolded by a blackbird. She told them she had been putting the finishing touches on the nest.

"Tsk, tsk! This nest belongs to me," the blackbird said disapprovingly.

The second backyard seemed charming, until a spirited dog ran around the corner, snapping at all the birds eating seeds at the feeder.

The third house wasn't any better. Two children with paintball guns sent yellow and blue paintball splatters in every direction. Mama had a near miss with the yellow paintball causing her to gasp, "I could have been turned canary yellow!"

The fourth house, 11 Holly Drive, had a very large backyard filled with colorful trumpet vines, a hummingbirds' favorite. Pecan trees offered nuts that would drop in the fall season, the harvest available for pecan pies and pralines. Honeysuckle grew all around the freshly painted white picket fence. There was a stone birdbath, a two-story wooden playhouse, and a small stream that flowed behind the fence. Rows of bird feeders, with a variety of seeds and sugar water, hung from a string of twine.

Behind the flowers, a small wooden birdhouse clung to the side of the playhouse. An elderly couple crouched near the fence, planting more honeysuckle. The yard smelled of a variety of things, including honey, fresh paint, cedar, and summer time. All the smells combined gave the whole backyard a feeling of time standing still. The Humming family knew they had finally reached a place where they would be okay. A place to call home.

In the couple of years that passed, Hanna was often sick and weak. She had frequent doctor appointments. One particular day, Doctor Redbird told the Humming family that Hanna had a rare bird disease. The Hummings were heartbroken but they remained positive and continued to follow their doctor's orders. Because of her disease and having only one wing, Hanna was kept close, often not even allowed to spend her day outside with her big brother Henry. This made Hanna and Henry very sad.

Henry, wanting to lift Hanna's spirits, promised to teach her how to fly one day. Hanna spent time drawing pictures of herself in flight with Henry. In her pictures, she was happy and healthy. She imagined that when she was happy, healthy, and able to fly, that she would never, ever go back inside. She would eat outside, bathe outside, sleep outside, and fly outside.

One early morning, Henry was jotting down Hanna's progress in a notebook. Hanna was using the thermometer as a baton. Hanna twirled the thermometer with her one wing, tossed it up in the air, and attempted to catch it. She missed, and it landed on Henry's notebook, causing him to huff in irritation.

"Hanna, stop playing around and put that in your beak," Henry scolded.

Hanna sighed and took the thermometer back, placing it in her beak. Henry went back to writing, but he couldn't help the thoughts that popped into his head: "She's bored. She's tired of being in bed, and you promised her a day outside." Henry shook the thoughts away. He was trying to help her get better by making sure she followed Doctor Redbird's advice to the letter. Once he managed that, he would take her outside and teach her how to fly.

"You took your multivitamin at eight o' clock. I gave you five droppers of nectar an hour ago. Yep, it's time for more nectar," Henry said.

The thermometer beeped, and Henry took it from Hanna's beak. He wrote one hundred and five degrees in his notebook with a satisfied smile.

Hanna sat up. "Take me outside. I want to feel the breeze on my face and smell the trumpet vines. I want to visit with the other birds. Maybe you could start giving me those flying lessons. You promised, remember?"

Henry put his notebook down and grabbed the dropper. He filled it with red nectar. He held it to Hanna's beak. Hanna drank from the dropper dutifully.

"Once Doctor Redbird confirms how much better you're doing, I will teach you how to fly. I promise," Henry reassured her.

"What if he doesn't have good news?" she worried.

"He will. We've been doing everything he suggested and more. You have to be optimistic."

Hanna nodded. "No matter what he says, I think it's time to tell the bird community about my sickness. Especially Jay-Jay and Stella. They think we go to Doctor Redbird and take all these precautions because of my one wing. If they knew, they would understand and help."

"Help? We don't need charity. They will make a big deal of it and poke their beaks where they don't belong. We can do this as a family. Besides, tomorrow Doctor Redbird will look at your scans and tell us the disease is gone. There will be nothing to tell," Henry said.

The next morning was humid and rainy. Henry helped Hanna out of her nest. They waited outside on one of the wooden planks of the playhouse while Papa and Mama got ready. They watched the raindrops sprinkle into the birdbath. Henry felt the warm weight of Hanna against his wing as she leaned on him for support. Hanna was particularly weak that morning.

Henry tried to think of a joke or a hopeful quote to tell his sister, but nothing came to mind. Papa and Mama joined them. Together, they flew through the rain to Doctor Redbird's tree office for Hanna's monthly checkup.

As he always did, Henry held Hanna's wing throughout the blood work and scan. Henry knew Hanna would never get used to the needle they used to take her blood. Hanna giggled as Henry made silly faces. Doctor Redbird left the room. They waited in silence for the results.

Finally, the door opened and Doctor Redbird walked into the room with Hanna's scans. He looked worried and sad. Henry hugged Hanna close. Papa and Mama glanced at each other.

"What is it, Doctor? Is something wrong?" Papa asked.

"Bob. Bonnie. After looking at Hanna's scan, I'm sorry to say the disease has spread."

"Will I die?" Hanna asked.

Doctor Redbird paused a moment before shaking his head and replying, "Let's think positive. Hanna, I need you to take these vitamins and minerals every day and rest as much as possible," Doctor Redbird said.

Hanna looked at Henry. "I'm tired of resting," she said, looking at Papa and Mama. "I want to go outside with Henry. Tell them, Henry. Tell them how you're going to teach me how to fly."

"Why would you tell your sister this knowing she has one wing?" Mama asked Henry in her most stern voice.

"Owen Owl says if you put your mind to something, you can do anything you want," Henry replied.

Doctor Redbird patted Henry on the back. "I can see some truth to that, but medically speaking, Hanna will need her rest. I'd like to see her back in two weeks."

"Yes, Doctor," Papa said as he took Mama's wing in his own.

Henry gave Hanna an encouraging smile even though deep down he'd like to tell Doctor Redbird that he was wrong, that Hanna wasn't sick and didn't need rest. He would also like to add that they did everything he said so how could she not be better. He wanted to ask for a miracle cure, but he knew there was no such thing. But most of all, he wanted a moment to himself to have a good cry. Instead, he smiled, listened to the doctor's orders, and whispered a prayer. He then swore to himself he would take care of Hanna as he always did.

Hanna tugged on Henry's right wing and motioned for him to come closer. She whispered, "Don't worry, Henry. I have a plan."

Fun Fact: Hummingbirds choose safe, sheltered locations for their nests, ensuring that their hatchlings are protected from sun, wind, rain, or predators.

CHAPTER TWO

Happy Birthday - One Week Later

Henry flew out of his wooden birdhouse and landed on the bird feeder next to three red cardinals. It was a warm, peaceful day and Henry felt it was specially made for him. He felt different today, wiser perhaps. He grinned.

The peaceful moment came to an abrupt halt when a loud screech pierced their ears and was followed by a rough landing. The bird feeder swung high and the three cardinals flew away.

Henry looked at his best friend, Jay-Jay. "Must you let out that loud screech every time?" he asked.

"Happy Birthday, Henry!" Jay-Jay said. "Eight years: it's a good age. But being ten, I have to say I got the better end of the deal."

Henry smiled. His friend Jay-Jay was full of himself but he meant well. Jay-Jay, a blue jay, was a beautiful shade of blue on the bulk of his body but had the traditional shades of blue on his top and back feathers with white and black peeking out beneath. His beak was a strong, sturdy black.

"Did your mama make honeysuckle cake for your birthday?"

"Yep. For the eighth year in a row."

Jay-Jay rubbed his belly and did a silly dance of twists, turns, and one backward flip.

Stella, their friend and neighbor, landed on the birdbath below them. She didn't seem to notice Henry and Jay-Jay. She was a yellow finch with dark colored wings that had one bright white line going across the span of them. Her eyes were large and focused. Stella studied the water in the birdbath carefully before placing one leg in it. A look of satisfaction crossed her face and she settled into the birdbath. Stella bathed, flapped, and dried off in the sun.

"One," Stella said aloud.

Jay-Jay whispered to Henry, "Here she goes."

Stella repeated the process of bathing.

"Two," Stella said aloud.

Jay-Jay smothered a laugh with his wing as Henry flew over to Stella.

"Hi, Stella," Henry greeted her. "You look clean to me."

"One moment, Henry."

Stella tested the water for the third time and settled in. When she finished she dried herself in the sun.

"Three, and done! Happy Birthday, Henry!" Stella chirped with a smile.

"Thank you." Henry stopped hovering and landed next to her on the birdbath. Jay-Jay joined them.

Stella flew over to inspect the birdseed. She carefully plucked out certain seeds and flew back to the birdbath to wash each one vigorously.

"You really need to see Doctor Redbird about your OCD, Stella. Those seeds are perfectly fine," Jay-Jay scolded.

Stella paid no attention to Jay-Jay's words as she lined her seeds up in rows of five. Only then did she begin to eat them.

"We're heading to my house in a bit for honeysuckle cake. Will you come?" Henry asked Stella.

"I wouldn't miss it for the world! I have a present for you, Henry," Stella said.

Stella flew over to the window ledge of the humans' house and returned with a small package that she handed to Henry. She washed her wings before returning to eat her seeds. Henry opened the wrapping quickly. Twine landed on Jay-Jay's head. He frowned and flicked it off in irritation.

"Stella, I love it!" Henry gleefully held up his new backpack. It was a sturdy backpack made of burlap with two perfectly sized straps to hold it on his tiny back.

"You can hold plenty of seeds in there. I counted three times to make sure!" Stella said proudly.

"Aren't you going to tell him how you managed to make such a pack?" Jay-Jay asked.

Stella narrowed her eyes in irritation.

"Jay-Jay took scraps from the humans' house. I put them together to make it, though. But don't worry, I sanitized everything," Stella assured him.

"And I still have my own present for you," Jay-Jay said proudly.

"Y'all are the best," Henry said with a smile.

"Stating the obvious," Jay-Jay replied.

Stella started scratching like crazy. Henry took notice. Jay-Jay backed away from her.

"I can't stop itching. Something's happening. I think I'm getting a rash," Stella cried in a panic.

"Because you bathe three times a day, Miss OCD," Jay-Jay told her.

"Let's go see Doctor Redbird," Henry said.

Stella started scratching her back, then her head.

"I'll see Owen Owl. He has more southern hospitality," Stella said, continuing to scratch. "Will y'all come with me?"

"Of course," Henry chimed.

Jay-Jay took a moment and then finally said, "I guess, just don't fly too close to me. In case it's contagious."

Stella rolled her eyes and the trio took off toward Owen Owl's lab.

When they arrived, Owen Owl quickly guided them into his personal room of remedies. Owen Owl wore eyeglasses and a tie-dyed bandanna. He examined Stella's mysterious itching feathers. Henry stood close to Stella for moral support, something he was quite used to doing for Hanna. Jay-Jay nosily peered into Owen Owl's cabinets. Jay-Jay lifted a clear bottle filled with a strange black, tar-like substance.

"What's this?" Jay-Jay asked uncorking the lid and taking a whiff.

Owen Owl pushed his eyeglasses up the bridge of his nose, "I wouldn't . . . "

Jay-Jay let a small drop fall on a feather from his wing.

" . . . do that," Owen Owl finished but not soon enough.

Jay-Jay tried to wipe the black goo off but it wouldn't budge. Owen Owl grabbed a strip of material, applied it to the spot, and pulled.

Jay-Jay flew upward with a screech, hitting his head on the ceiling in the process. "That hurt like . . . "

"Wax," Owen Owl said. "For removing unwanted feathers or fur."

Jay-Jay rubbed his aching bare spot. "Why, just why? Who would do such a thing?"

Stella giggled, "That's about as useful as a roadmap with no street names."

Owen Owl went back to examining Stella. Jay-Jay continued to rub his aching wing. Owen Owl gave Stella's feathers a couple of taps and then nodded.

"I have just the thing. This is nothing more than dry feather, which is often accompanied by itch," Owen Owl explained.

"Told you Stella. Over bathing," Jay-Jay said.

"Thanks for the heads up Baldy," Stella teased.

Owen Owl looked through his cabinets, tossing items over his shoulder in an effort to find what he was looking for. Henry and Jay-Jay ducked out of the way to avoid being hit. Owen Owl turned around with a smile and a tube of cream labeled Pink Miracle Cream.

Henry wished that he could find such a cream to cure Hanna. Owen Owl uncapped the tube and gave it a pinch, offering it to Stella. Stella took the pinch of cream on her wing and rubbed it all over.

"I made this one myself. Stop tingle, prickle, and itch with just one pinch," Owen Owl chuckled proudly to himself.

Stella waited a moment. Henry didn't realize he was squeezing her wing in anticipation. He could use some good news for once. Stella smiled and Henry let out the air in his lungs that he hadn't even realized he'd been holding.

"Goodness gracious, it worked!" Stella exclaimed.

Henry felt as relieved as he imagined Stella felt until all of a sudden Stella's feathers slowly started turning pink right before his very eyes.

"Ah, Stella," Henry pointed.

Stella looked down. Her eyes widened in fear. "What's happening?" Stella asked before breaking into an uncontrollable fit of giggles.

Jay-Jay took several steps back until he was as far away as he could get. Henry had the opposite reaction and moved closer to her.

"What's happening to her?" Henry asked.

Owen Owl seemed unfazed and replied with a wave of his wing, "She's tickled pink. Common side effect."

Stella spoke between giggles, "What? I . . . can't . . . stop . . . laughing. Please . . . make . . . it . . . stop."

"All giggles aside. Pink is your color Stella," Jay-Jay offered encouragement from the far side of the room.

Henry was beside himself. "Help her!"

Owen Owl dug through his cabinets and pulled out several jars. He poured them into a bowl all at once and *boom*! There was a small explosion that left Jay-Jay with a mohawk and Henry's feathers askew.

Owen Owl poured the contents into a glass and handed it to Stella, "Drink this."

"Wait! Does that have . . . " Henry was too late.

Stella drank the entire glass.

" . . . Side effects?" Henry finished with a huff.

Stella stopped giggling and her feathers returned back to normal. Jay-Jay looked in the mirror and saw his mohawk.

"I like this look on me. As for you, Stella, I'm glad you're not giggling like a mad bird but you may want to consider the whole pink thing," Jay-Jay offered.

The trio thanked Owen Owl and headed back to the birdbath to relax.

"Henry! Time for cake!" Mama called.

Jay-Jay shrieked and flew off the birdbath with such force that the water splashed on Henry and Stella. Stella looked down in horror at her drenched feathers.

"He can be so rude sometimes! I'll be up in a minute," Stella told Henry.

Henry nodded and flew toward his birdhouse. He could hear Stella counting as he made his way inside.

Five minutes later, Henry and Mama sat around a table made of pinecones and tree bark. Papa carried Hanna into the room and placed her on a chair made of bent reeds. Stella, Jay-Jay and his parents stood to the side waiting to sing. A honeysuckle cake sat on the center of the table with the words *"Happy Birthday Henry!"* written in nectar. Trumpet vine flowers draped the sides of the cake in place of icing.

Hanna sneaked a sip of juice from the trumpet vine.

"Wait, Hanna. Henry has to make a wish first," Mama said.

Henry smiled before blowing the flower out. A white thought-cloud formed over Henry's head: He imaged he was on a cruise with a tropical nectar drink in his wings. The scene in the cloud changed and he imagined himself on the Eiffel Tower in Paris. It changed again and he imagined flying over the ocean with a great big smile. The cloud over Henry's head faded away.

"Time to open presents," Mama said handing Henry the gifts.

Jay-Jay and his parents gave Henry a bronze compass that they found in the humans' office.

"I will put this compass in the backpack Stella gave me," Henry said.

Henry opened his gift from Mama and Papa. It was a book called *The Seeds of Life.* Owen Owl smiled and gave a thumbs-up on the front cover.

"It's packed with information on how a bird can make it in the big world. Owen Owl is the author," Papa told him.

Henry hugged the book to his chest feathers. "Thanks Papa, thanks Mama!"

"I will give you your gift later Henry. It's not ready yet," Hanna said.

"Cake time at last," Jay-Jay said as he rubbed his belly.

They all ate the sweet and delicious cake and then spoke about upcoming events.

"The weather will be cool soon and the humans will dress up in scary costumes and try to scare the weather back to being hot. I have no idea why they even bother. Every year they do that and every year the cold weather still comes," Mama said.

"Mama, can Jay-Jay and Stella sleep over?" Henry asked.

"It's okay with me if it's okay with your Papa," she replied.

"Well, since it's your birthday," Papa teased.

"Yay!" Henry, Jay-Jay, and Stella cheered.

Jay-Jay, Stella, Henry, and his family waved goodbye to Jay-Jay's parents. The star-filled sky shed light upon the trumpet vines that blew softly in the breeze. A flash of lightning followed by a roll of thunder warned of bad weather to come.

Fun Fact: An average hummingbird's heart beats more than 1,200 beats per minute.

CHAPTER THREE

The Storm

In the humans' living room, an older, white-haired man held his wife's hand as they watched the flat-screen television together on a tan couch. His wife wore a fluffy white robe and white rabbit slippers; she was petite and white-haired just like her husband. On the television, a news reporter explained about a hurricane in the Gulf, heading to the coast of Louisiana.

"It appears to be gaining strength, folks. For those of you who haven't evacuated, you are going to want to board up those windows and bring in the family pets if you haven't already done so. We are predicting the hurricane will reach the coast of Louisiana around two o'clock in the morning," the news reporter said.

The older man, Mr. Whitman, spoke to his wife: "We need to close the shutters, honey. This is one storm I wish we would have left for. You said you went to the store earlier for water and canned goods, right?"

"Yes, dear. Let's get those windows closed and put the generator in the laundry room," Mrs. Whitman replied.

The wind whipped through the yard. The trees, swings, and bird feeders swung back and forth. Two owls on a pine branch exchanged worried glances and flew off into the night. A flash of lightning illuminated the entire night sky and a roll of thunder followed behind.

Back inside the Humming's birdhouse, Hanna was snug in her tiny nest. A nest so small that only a single penny could fit inside. Henry sat beside that nest as Hanna presented a package for him.

"Open it," Hanna whispered with bright and eager eyes.

Henry tore the package open carefully and found a brown journal, a pot of ink, and one of Hanna's feathers.

"Hanna, I love it!" Henry told his sister.

"Jay-Jay helped me by gathering the scraps of paper and string to bind it together. He took the pot of ink from the humans. The feather is one of my own so when you hold it, you can think of me," Hanna explained.

"When I write in this journal, I will always think of you Hanna."

"Henry, I want you to go on your adventure. I want you to see the world like you've always wanted," Hanna told Henry. "I know you stay behind because I'm sick and I have one wing but you can't stay in one place forever. You have to see the world. I don't want to hold you back."

With her wing, Hanna wiped a tear that fell from her eye.

"I love this backyard; it's home," Henry said. "Besides, I wouldn't miss celebrating your birthday. You know Mama has a whole fun day planned this weekend for you. She loves to give us each our day."

"Henry, you belong out there in the world, exploring, meeting other birds, and writing about your adventures in your journal," Hanna persisted.

Hanna pushed the journal further into Henry's wings until it pressed firmly against his chest.

"Promise me," Hanna said. "That will be your gift to me for my birthday."

Henry wiped a tear from his eye. "I can't promise that."

Hanna sat up with determination.

"You have to go, Henry Humming. I will be the saddest hummingbird in the world if you do not promise me. There's something else that may persuade you," Hanna said.

Hanna handed Henry a small crumpled piece of paper. Henry opened the paper to see a list of items.

"What's this?" Henry asked.

"The plan; our plan. It's hope," Hanna offered.

"Where did you get this?" Henry asked.

"Owen Owl gave it to me. He says it's not easy to find the items but he cured himself of the bird disease many years ago with this exact cure," Hanna explained.

"Why didn't Doctor Redbird mention this to Papa or Mama?" Henry asked.

"Not many believe in the cure. Plus, like Owen Owl said, it's not easy. It's dangerous even," Hanna said.

Henry glanced over the list. Some of the items, like Redwood bark, lavender oil, and cactus prickles, seemed easy enough. However, Henry stopped and reread the last a few items to make sure his eyes weren't playing tricks on him. Nope, it was written in bold black ink. Henry read no further.

"I don't know, Hanna. Owen Owl turned Stella pink and almost blew up his whole nest. I'm not sure he knows as much as Doctor Redbird. Plus, it will take time; what if I can't find some of these? What if I don't make it back in time and you–"

"Die? If you don't go I will die anyway. If you go, maybe you won't make it in time. *But*, if you do come back with the cure, I may live a long life. At least the second option is hope," Hanna encouraged.

Henry looked down at the journal and then Hanna's feather. He saw an inscription for the first time on the journal. It read, "To my dear brother Henry Humming. Have your adventure! Love, Hanna Humming."

"Okay Hanna, I will think about it," Henry promised.

Hanna smiled, "That's all I'm asking. Thank you."

Henry flitted back to his bedroom. He settled into his nest while Jay-Jay and Stella got into their bigger nests on each side of him. Jay-Jay's nest was haphazardly put together with twigs, grass, and leaves, which poked out in every direction. Stella's nest, the direct opposite, was neatly put together in a perfect circle; nothing was out of place.

"How do I look, y'all?" Jay-Jay asked.

Stella plucked an imaginary needle. "We are going to bed; what does it matter what you look like?"

"It matters if you want to get some sleep tonight. You look very handsome, Jay-Jay," Henry said.

"Now that's a real friend. Stella you could learn a thing or two from Henry," Jay-Jay said.

Stella rolled her eyes and turned over in her nest. Jay-Jay settled back down in his own nest.

"Goodnight," Henry said, hoping he could get some sleep and not fret about the list Hanna gave him.

Henry fluttered his wings and the fireflies moved away from the window, leaving the room dark save for the bright moon outside gleaming in the window. A flash of lightning lit the room and Stella pulled some of her pine needles from her nest on top of her.

The wind picked up and a downpour of rain began. The thunder rolled right behind it. A loud cracking sound, followed by a sound similar to a train, began to roar louder and louder. Henry, Jay-Jay, and Stella jumped in fright and sat straight up in their nests. The wooden birdhouse began to shake, making a rattling sound. Rain started to come in the small wooden hole that served as a window in Henry's room.

One room over, Hanna stirred in her nest. The wind picked up and her room made a rattling sound.

"Papa! Mama!" Hanna called out. "Henry!"

Mama and Papa flew into Hanna's room. "Hurry. Get on my back," Papa told Hanna.

"Let's go get Henry, Jay-Jay, and Stella," Mama said.

Back in Henry's room, Henry worried about his sister. Hanna could never sleep well during storms. "I'm going to check on Hanna," Henry said.

Jay-Jay and Stella nodded but before Henry could get halfway out of his nest, the birdhouse was shaken so violently that his bedroom was torn from the rest of the birdhouse. A gaping hole showed part of Hanna's room and his parents' room. Henry tried to call out to them but his voice was lost in the loud storm winds. The last image of his family was of Hanna on Papa's back and Mama's fearful eyes watching helplessly as Henry's room pulled away from the rest of the house.

Henry, Jay-Jay, and Stella screamed as Henry's bedroom spun in a cyclone of rotating wind and rain. Henry put his wings out; Jay-Jay grabbed one and Stella grabbed the other. Together, the three birds held onto each other as Henry's room was carried far away.

As the cyclone force winds dissipated, Henry's room descended, tumbling sideways through cypress tree limbs and embedding in a long hanging cluster of Spanish moss. The moss caught them like a softball in a padded catcher's mitt and cushioned their landing. However, the moss didn't hold tight to the room for long. They slipped down to the moss's dangling end, landing softly on a floating swamp log. As they congratulated themselves on their good fortune, the log started drifting away. Henry got a better look and realized they were not on a log. They had landed onto the back of an alligator in the swamp. The alligator dove under the water and Henry's room began to sink. Jay-Jay screeched. Right before the house went completely under water, a duck hunter came out of the bayou blowing his duck whistle. A flock of ducks flew toward the sound. One of the ducks legs got caught on the looped knob of Henry's room and flew upward, bringing Henry's room with him. Jay-Jay screamed as if he was being waxed again. Henry and Stella stayed in quiet shock, frozen in fear.

The duck, not enjoying the weight of the birdhouse nor Jay-Jay's screams, panicked and shook free of the bird room. Henry's bedroom began to fall and landed in the back of a dump truck that was crossing the state line of Texas into New Mexico. They looked around to see they had landed on top of a huge pile of dirt in the truck. They waited for another incident in silence. Sometime in the night, the steady sound of the highway lulled the trio to sleep. Henry woke a few times during the night and remembered he wasn't home. He would glance over at Jay-Jay and Stella and a small feeling of relief would fill him knowing that he wasn't alone. One time, he woke and could see nothing but the stars in the night sky. He stared at them for a while and listened to Jay-Jay's snores. Another time he woke, he felt a cool breeze and there was a strong smell of saltwater in the air.

The next morning, Henry woke first. He saw that they were traveling on a bridge. A small crack in the dump truck revealed the light changing the colors of the ocean from green to blue. Henry had never seen water that stretched so far; there seemed to be no end. He looked upward and saw white birds circling above. A flash of green appeared in the crack and Henry tried to read the sign but failed. He didn't know it but they were traveling on Highway One north to south along California's beautiful coastal cliff line. The two-lane highway zig-zagging, rising, and falling around coves and curving around hillside slopes. Below the cliffs, small beach shops ran along a boardwalk. Swells from the Pacific ocean crashed onto the sandy beaches. There were surfers riding waves that gave them the magical feeling of "flying".

Henry was in shock yesterday, but today he was ready to figure out a way to get them home. So many thoughts were running through his mind: Did his parents and Hanna make it out of the birdhouse in time? Would he and his friends find their way back home? And if they could get back home, what would home look like after the storm damage?

Jay-Jay and Stella woke. Jay-Jay glanced through the hole and saw the surfers with their arms outstretched riding the waves. "Y'all have got to see this. Humans are flying. Or at least they're trying. They won't get far without wings."

Henry was about to tell them his plan but, before he could, the dump truck took a sharp turn, running over a huge bump. Henry's room flew up and out of the truck, and they landed in an ocean. A salty wave splashed against Henry's room soaking them. Jay-Jay screeched and fainted.

Fun Fact: Hummingbirds get the energy they need to maintain their metabolism primarily from flower nectar and hummingbird feeders.

CHAPTER FOUR

California - I See the Light

The sun caused the white sand to glisten like tiny shards of glass. The ocean was a deep blue and many white seagulls sat around it. A nearby sign read: "Welcome to California."

Henry, Jay-Jay, and Stella stared at the sign from Henry's bedroom, which had washed up onto the sand after taking quite a ride on a giant wave.

"California!" Henry shouted.

Jay-Jay covered his ears. "Seriously, don't scream. My ears are killing me right now."

"I wonder why," Stella said sarcastically.

Without warning, a huge wave crashed into the beach and pulled Henry's room back into the ocean. Jay-Jay screamed obnoxiously. Stella and Henry covered their sore ears. A seagull that had been watching the three new birds, flew toward them and tried to lift the room out of the ocean.

Several other gulls flew over to help. Together, the seagulls lifted the wooden bedroom out of the ocean and onto the middle of the beach sand, far from the ocean waves.

Henry flew out of his nest and lifted up his backpack from under the needles. He placed The Seeds of Life book from his parents and the journal Hanna gave him in the backpack, as well as Hanna's feather, the pot of ink, and compass. He peeked inside the journal and saw the list. He closed the backpack and put it around his wings, patting it reassuringly. Henry flew out of his room and onto the sand. Jay-Jay and Stella followed.

"Thank you for saving us," Henry said to the seagulls.

"I can't believe we are in California!" Jay-Jay said.

"This isn't good, this isn't good, this isn't good!" Stella paced nervously.

"Calm down, we need to think," Henry said.

"Dude, who are you guys?" the biggest seagull asked.

Henry, Jay-Jay, and Stella studied the seagull more closely. He had a yellow bill with a black ring, yellow legs, brown eyes, and a rounded head. His body was mostly white except for the gray back and upper wings.

"Not going to answer after I saved you guys? Tourists! My name is Surf. I'm the best surfer on the coast," Surf the seagull said.

"My name is Henry and these are my friends Jay-Jay and Stella," Henry told Surf.

"Where you dudes from?"

"Louisiana," Stella answered.

"Come a long way, did ya," Surf said.

"The hurricane brought us. Actually the tornado made during the hurricane started it and then there was an alligator, this duck, and a dump truck. I blame them all," Jay-Jay said a bit winded.

"We need to get back home to our families and let them know we are okay. We need to know that they are okay as well," Henry said.

"You have a long way to go, my friends. Of course you know that from migrating, so no worries," Surf said.

"Actually, we've never migrated before or traveled anywhere outside of our backyard in Louisiana," Henry explained.

Surf couldn't believe his ears, "Dude, that's so not cool! Who ever heard of birds that don't migrate?"

Stella dusted off the sand in irritation. "Well, Henry's sister Hanna . . ."

"*Screech*!" Jay-Jay interrupted Stella. He pointed across the street from the beach. There was a café with outdoor seating.

"Look! There has to be a famous bird nearby. See all those blue jays swarming around? They're protecting someone," Jay-Jay explained.

Stella continued to work religiously to get the sand out of her feathers. "Jay-Jay, they're like you. Go talk to them. Ask them if they know of a place where we can get cleaned up."

"I'd rather find out who they're protecting," Jay-Jay said flying off toward the café.

"Jay-Jay! We do not have time for this. We need to find our way back home," Henry called to his friend.

Surf shook his head, "Tourists!"

Henry and Stella flew after Jay-Jay and landed on a brightly tiled tabletop outside the café. The group of blue jays hurried along the ground picking up crumbs left over from the previous diners. Jay-Jay stood proudly before them.

"What are y'all doing?" Jay-Jay asked.

One of the taller blue jays pushed Jay-Jay aside. "Move sir. She will be here any minute."

"Who?" Henry, Jay-Jay, and Stella asked.

The blue jay didn't answer them. Another pack of blue jays flew in and then apart to let a lovely sparrow bird eat the collected crumbs.

"Who . . . is . . . that?" Henry asked in awe of the sparrow's beauty.

The sparrow walked over to Henry. Stella's beak dropped open in shock.

"I'm Britney Sparrow."

Stella finally found her voice and ranted on and on in excitement, "The famous singer bird, Britney Sparrow! I have all of your songs memorized. I sing them in the birdbath all the time. My favorites are "Oops! . . . I Tweeted Again," "Touch of My Wing," "Birdinizer," and "Fly Until the World Ends!"

"So it's *your* fault Stella thinks she can sing in the birdbath," Jay-Jay accused Britney.

Stella turned bright red. Britney grinned and looked back at Henry with a smile.

"Hanna will love to hear about us meeting Britney Sparrow," Stella told Henry.

"That's his little sister, not girlfriend," Jay-Jay added.

"Handsome Henry. I tell you what, Henry; I'd love to have lunch with you. Would you join me?" Britney asked.

Stella became a little jealous, "Oh, we don't have time. Right, Henry?"

"Huh?" Henry asked.

Henry remained frozen in place so Jay-Jay pushed him toward the crumbs. Stella moved forward and looked at Henry in disbelief.

"Henry, you shouldn't eat crumbs off the table. You're use to the seeds back home. You know, the ones that haven't been touched and contaminated by several other beaks," Stella said.

Jay-Jay pushed Stella aside and said to Britney: "Henry will gladly accept your offer."

Britney Sparrow smiled and motioned for him to dig in.

"Can my friends join us?" Henry asked.

"Sure," Britney said.

Stella watched in anger as Britney pushed Henry's feathers back and smiled at him. Stella refused to eat with them.

After they ate, Britney said, "Well I have a show to do but it was lovely meeting you!"

"Wait! Would you sign my journal?" Henry asked.

"Of course!" Britney signed the journal.

"Thank you! You have no idea how much this will mean to Hanna," Henry said with a smile.

Britney kissed the top of Henry's head and then moved backward until she was surrounded by the blue jays once more. They all flew off.

Henry hovered in the air, doing a little happy dance, the dance hummers do when in love.

Stella steamed in anger.

The open sign on the café came on and people walked off the street and into the café. A few windows were opened and a television was turned on. The sounds of the television drifted onto the patio outside, catching the attention of Henry, Jay-Jay, and Stella.

They flew inside the café unseen, landing on a bright orange tabletop. On the television, a news reporter talked about the damage the hurricane caused in Louisiana. The news reporter stood near the Whitman's, the elderly couple that owned the house where Henry, Jay-Jay, and Stella lived. The three of them crowded close together and listened nervously.

"Hello everyone. Thank you for tuning in. We are here today after the aftermath of the hurricane with Mr. and Mrs. Whitman. It is no secret that this hurricane will haunt us for many years after all the damage and lives lost. Please, Mr. and Mrs. Whitman, tell us about your experience and loss," the news reporter said.

Mr. Whitman spoke first. "We boarded up the windows and went to bed. I had my hearing aids off but my wife woke me to put them back in. I heard wind so loud I thought a train was roaring through our bedroom. The rain was pelting against the windows. I was sure it would come through the boards and glass."

"Tell us why you didn't evacuate when everyone was warned to do so," the news reporter asked.

Mrs. Whitman answered, "We have been through many hurricanes and we got through them just fine. We never imagined this much damage would come to our home and yard. The tornadoes brought on by the hurricane didn't help matters."

"Could you walk us through the backyard first and then through your home?" the news reporter suggested.

The news reporter and the Whitman's walked toward the backyard. Henry, Jay-Jay, and Stella glanced at each other in fear and anticipation. The news camera zoomed in on a section of the yard.

They gasped at what they saw. The playhouse was turned upside-down. Henry flew closer to the television to get a better look. Jay-Jay and Stella followed him.

"Where is the birdhouse? Where are my parents? Where's Hanna? Do you see anyone?" Henry asked one question after the other.

The news reporter's camera pulled away from the damage and back to the elderly couple.

Mr. Whitman said, "When we stepped out the door and saw our backyard damaged and destroyed, we cried. I built that wooden playhouse for my children, and my grandchildren love that playhouse. The flower gardens, all destroyed. Our bird feeders . . ."

Mr. Whitman stopped to dry some tears. His wife grabbed his hand and gave it a reassuring pat. Henry's heart sank, a lump formed in his throat and awful thoughts flooded his mind.

The reporter spoke into the camera: "As you can see folks, everyone is feeling the devastation of this hurricane. We will not forget anytime soon the heartbreak left behind by this storm."

The news camera showed one last glimpse of the backyard. Henry, Jay-Jay, and Stella pressed closer to the television. Half of a bird nest floated by in a puddle.

"My nest! That's my home!" Stella cried. "Where are my parents? Do you think they're still alive? Do you think they blew away like we did? Where are they?"

The camera went back to the news reporter. A butterfly photobombed the reporter, flying over her head with her tongue sticking out. The reporter said, "We will return with more footage in a moment."

A commercial began. Henry, Jay-Jay, and Stella stared at the television in disbelief.

"This is unbelievable," Stella said with a sniff.

"Not really. I know that butterfly; she's obnoxious," Jay-Jay said.

"I'm talking about the damage to our yard, bird brain," Stella said.

"I didn't get to see my nest. Do y'all think it's still there?" Jay-Jay asked.

Henry and Stella remained silent. One of the waiters walked up to the television and changed the channel.

"That's too depressing," the waiter said.

"No!" Henry, Jay-Jay, and Stella squawked.

"How will we know if our families are okay?" Henry questioned.

"What if my parents are in that dirty ditch in the back, trapped with no way of getting out or getting clean?' Stella added.

"Maybe our parents are trying to find scraps to rebuild. That's got to be why we didn't see them," Jay-Jay tried hard to think positive.

"Or they're injured and need our help," Henry said with concern.

Henry, Jay-Jay, and Stella flew out of the cafe and back to the beach.

"What if Hanna's all alone? She can't fend for herself!" Henry wondered aloud.

"Other birds would help her," Stella said to try to comfort him.

"What if no one survived except Hanna?" Henry said.

"No way my parents didn't make it through that, Jays are tough," Jay-Jay stated.

"Drama birds! The casting call's over on Sunset Boulevard. You three will be a seed-in," Surf said as he landed near them.

"No one asked your opinion," Jay-Jay said to Surf.

"We have to find our way home and fast," Henry said.

"You three need to live a little. Get a life! If your family is in trouble, and they might not be, what good will it do to rush home? Instead, make the most of this and bring back some supplies they may need," Surf lectured.

Henry stared at Surf. Surf's words reminded Henry of Hanna's request. The list, the cure, supplies, a life, Henry thought all at once.

"Supplies? A life?" Henry said nodding his head in agreement.

"Yes, get a life. *Live*!" Surf encouraged again.

Henry pulled his backpack around and took out the list Hanna gave him for the cure.

"What's that?" Jay-Jay asked.

Henry folded the list back and put it in his backpack. He didn't want Jay-Jay and Stella to know of Hanna's sickness or the list. Not yet anyway.

"Surf, do you have something I can put some of that ocean water in?" Henry asked.

Surf took off one of the necklaces from around his neck. The cord was made of twine with a small charm that happened to be an empty clear glass bottle with a cork on top.

"Will this work?" Surf asked.

Henry's eyes lit up with joy. "Perfect."

Jay-Jay scratched his head in confusion. "What are you doing?"

"Getting a life," Henry said as he flew over to the ocean waters and hovered above them.

Surf followed. "Allow me," Surf said, offering Henry his help.

Henry nodded. Surf took the cork off and scooped some salty ocean water into the glass bottle and put the cork back on before handing it over to Henry. Henry and Surf flew back to where Jay-Jay and Stella waited with puzzled looks on their faces.

"A souvenir?" Jay-Jay questioned.

"Souvenir, supplies. It won't hurt to grab a few things along the way as long as we keep moving toward home," Henry said with a smile. For the first time in a long time Henry felt hopeful.

Fun Fact: When nectar is scarce, hummingbirds will also feed on tree sap.

CHAPTER FIVE

Meet Emmett

A forest filled with tall redwood trees loomed above the three little birds. They stared in awe. Next to these giant trees they appeared to be mere crumbs if one were to look down from the highest branch. Henry shook himself out of the wonderment daze. He knew he had to collect the items for the cure and he wanted to be swift about it as to not dilly-dally too long in any one place.

"This can't be the right way. Where are we?" Henry wondered aloud as he pulled out the compass from his backpack. "How do I use this thing anyway?" Henry shook the compass vigorously.

"Maybe I should lead," Jay-Jay said.

"Y'all, look at these trees!" Stella said still staring in amazement.

Henry put the compass back in his backpack and pulled out and opened *The Seeds of Life.*

"*The Seeds of Life* calls these redwood trees. Oh my gosh, these are the redwood trees. This is right," Henry said slamming the book closed and tossing it back in his backpack. "I need some bark."

"Huh? What for?" Jay-Jay questioned.

"Oh, ah, a souvenir," Henry stumbled over his lie. Henry glanced around and saw a redwood branch on the ground. He flew over to examine it. Stella and Jay-Jay followed.

Before Stella and Jay-Jay could question Henry's strange souvenir, a swoosh of black and purple feathers flew so close to their heads, they had to duck down or they would be hit by the flying bird. Unfortunately for Henry, he did not duck down fast enough and the swoosh collided into him, knocking him over.

"Rough landing, rough landing. Sorry about that. The name is Emmett. What's your name, son?" Emmett asked Henry, who was still rubbing his head.

"Henry. You're a—"

"Black-chinned hummer," Emmett finished Henry's sentence.

"Right," Henry agreed.

Emmett moved so close to Henry, his beak pressed against Henry's beak. Emmett squinted his eyes to get a better look. He moved his neck side to side and it cracked both times.

"Oh, oh that felt good. These old bones aren't what they used to be. What's your daddy's name, son?" Emmett asked Henry.

Henry was about to answer but Emmett continued on, "Gregory Humming?"

"No, it's—"

Again, Emmett cut Henry off. "You aren't Gregory's boy?"

Henry let out an irritated puff and backed away from Emmett's hard stare. "No. My father is Bob Humming. I'm Henry Humming."

Henry turned back to the bark, irritated at having been bumped into and then interrogated. Jay-Jay flexed his muscles and moved toward the bark.

"Allow me, Henry. This job requires strength and endurance, the two things jays excel at," Jay-Jay boasted.

Henry nodded and watched with great humor as Jay-Jay groaned and strained to break off a piece of redwood bark to no avail.

"You're doing it all wrong, son. Let me show you how it's done," Emmett told Jay-Jay.

"You? You're older than dirt," Jay-Jay said. Jay-Jay got back to working on the bark. He groaned, he strained, he wiped sweat from his feathers, and he groaned and strained some more. Finally, Jay-Jay slumped down in exhaustion.

"Just . . . need . . . a . . . minute, "Jay-Jay said, gasping for air.

All of a sudden, a woodpecker swooped in, landed on the branch, and began pecking. Several pieces of bark flew from the branch, raining down all around Henry, Jay-Jay, Stella, and Emmett. The woodpecker looked up to see he had an audience and flew off. Jay-Jay gathered a few pieces of the fallen bark and offered it to Henry.

"I loosened it for him," Jay-Jay said.

Henry grinned and took the bark. "Of course you did." Henry placed the bark pieces into his backpack and zipped it back up.

"This reminds me of when I was a young chap much like yourself and went around collecting nature pieces," Emmett said.

"We need to get going," Henry said looking at his friends. He was ready to move forward and get that much closer to home.

Fun Fact: The blue jay with its bold colors, and even bolder personality, is one of the most common and familiar backyard birds in the eastern United States.

CHAPTER SIX

The Flight Fight: Henry versus Slade

As they flew over a field with very few bushes, Emmett, slightly breathless, joined them in flight.

"You almost lost me back there. You three are bringing back my youth," Emmett stated happily.

"I'm sorry; why are you still here?" Jay-Jay asked.

"What's that, son? You have to speak louder. Old Emmett's ears aren't what they used to be," Emmett said to Jay-Jay.

A loud screech filled the air causing them to jump.

"Now I can hear you," Emmett said.

"Wasn't me. That's louder than my warning call," Jay-Jay said.

They looked up to see a huge predator bird circling above them.

"Fly for cover. Now!" Emmett yelled.

They flew to a bush in the middle of the field. The sun was going down and the moon was coming up. Henry, Jay-Jay, Stella, and Emmett huddled together under the small bush that had hardly any leaves on it.

"What kind of bird are we hiding from?" Stella asked.

"That would be a golden eagle. I've seen one attack and eat a full-grown deer before. We would simply be an appetizer. His second important food source is other birds," Emmett answered.

Henry pulled out *The Seeds of Life.* He flipped to the golden eagle page and read, "The golden eagle has very good eyesight, spots prey from a long distance, and is eight times more powerful than a human in resolving power."

"What does that mean?" Stella asked.

"Speak bird! Speak bird!" Jay-Jay said frantically.

"Golden eagles can make out objects faster than humans. It means the few leaves on this bush are not nearly enough to hide us. We have to get out of here; standing still will make no difference," Henry explained.

"I wouldn't recommend that, son. Golden eagles can fly fifty miles per hour," Emmett warned.

"How do you know that?" Henry asked.

"You don't live this long and not learn a thing or two. Let me recall the last time, oh yes, it was back in—"

Jay-Jay threw his wings in the air. "Really? Story time? Between Henry's book and this old geezer's stories, how will we have time to discuss our favorite seeds?" Jay-Jay said sarcastically.

Emmett leaned closer to Jay-Jay's beak, "What's that, son? You want to talk about seed? We should focus on the problem at hand first. That eagle."

Jay-Jay slapped his face in astonishment. They all turned their attention back to the golden eagle.

"I'm going out. I'll fly south, y'all start flying west as fast as y'all can," Henry said.

Stella grabbed Henry's wing. "What? Are you crazy? You're going to get yourself killed."

"Let's not be too hasty, son. I can handle this. You three whippersnappers head on out," Emmett said.

Jay-Jay glared at Emmett. "Listen Grandpa—"

Stella let go of Henry and turned to Jay-Jay, "Jay-Jay! I think we should all work together."

Jay-Jay sighed but nodded in agreement. They all turned around to make sure Henry agreed but the space was empty. Henry had flown out already. Stella, Jay-Jay, and Emmett looked up through the bare branched bush to see the golden eagle diving straight their way. Just before it looked like he would join them in the bush, he changed paths.

That's when they saw Henry doing circles around the eagle's head. Henry dove down, then up and hovered in the air waiting for the eagle to follow. The eagle charged full speed toward Henry.

"You're messing with the wrong bird, Hummer. I will catch you and make you watch as I eat your friends and then I'll eat you for dessert," the golden eagle said.

Henry wasn't fazed by the threat. He remained hovering in the air. "My name is Henry not Hummer."

"My name is Slade and that will be the last name you hear," Slade told Henry.

Stella cried out for Henry to move as Slade closed in on him. Henry flew sideways and out of the way in the nick of time. Henry sighed in relief as Slade flew right past him, barely missing a tree along the forest's edge.

Slade, not giving up, started angrily flying back toward Henry.

Henry watched as Slade flew higher and higher. Henry knew Slade would try to dive on him.

Slade dove down and just inches before he reached Henry, Henry flew backward. Slade almost landed head-first in the ground.

Henry teased Slade by making circles around his head. Angered, Slade flew toward Henry and made another side move. Slade tried to fly around Henry and dive again. Henry flew backward and then hovered right above Slade.

Slade took a deep breath and smiled an evil smile. He flew toward Henry at fifty miles per hour. Henry dove sideways and down as fast as he could. Slade smiled and followed Henry down toward the ground. Slade believed he had Henry trapped.

"You're going to taste so good as my after-dinner mint," Slade said to Henry.

Inches before Henry hit the ground, he turned up and made a loud whistle while coming up in the air really high, a common move for a hummer. Slade, unable to stop fast enough, landed beak-first in the dirt.

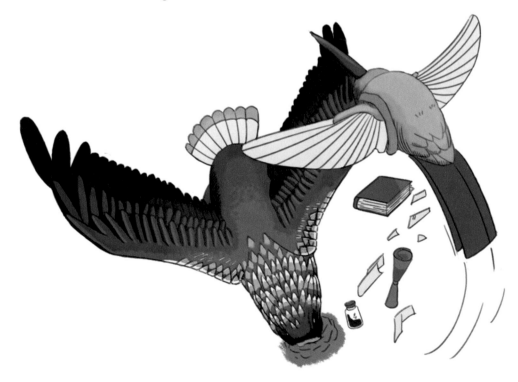

Henry swung back around and hovered over Slade. The items along with the list for the cure fell out of Henry's backpack and landed in front of Slade. Slade stared at the list with great interest.

"*Henry!*" Stella screamed.

Henry heard Stella's scream and loud stomping. A herd of cattle wildly ran his way. Slade pushed with all his might against the dirt and flew away. Henry snatched his items and list and flew up just in time. The herd of cattle stampeded through the field followed by a barking border collie.

Jay-Jay screeched and Stella flew over and hit Henry with her wing.

"You scared the salt out of me!" Stella scolded but then softened and said, "Give me some sugar."

Henry blushed as Stella kissed his cheek over and over. By the time she stopped, Henry felt dizzy.

Jay-Jay flew over to Henry with a huge smile. "You're either crazy or brave. I'm going with brave," Jay-Jay said, nudging Henry teasingly. "Now, let's get out of here!"

~Slade~

Several falcons surrounded Slade in a wine vineyard a couple of miles from where Henry had defeated him. Slade popped a large purple grape off one of the vines and tossed it into his beak. He slowly chewed before speaking to the falcons who waited to see what this meeting was all about.

"Welcome, falcons. My name is Slade. You must be wondering why I have gathered you here. For many years, my kind has talked about joining forces with the falcon. We have much in common. For example, small birds mean nothing but air food," Slade said to his captive audience.

The falcons looked at each other and nodded in agreement.

"Have you heard of the cure for the bird disease?" Slade asked them.

The falcons seemed confused.

Slade continued, "There's a rare bird disease going around and a list of ingredients that may cure this said disease. One of the ingredients happens to be a feather from an eagle. The Mob Boss himself knows of this cure and plans to bottle it himself. He will stop at nothing to be the provider of this cure. I say we stop him and any other bird with such plans. They will pluck us bald, steal our babies if they have to," Slade said.

One of the bigger falcons, Malcom, stepped forward. "What does this have to do with the falcons? Why should we get involved?" Malcom asked.

"When the eagle feathers become scarce, who do you think they will go after? I've heard the rumors and all beaks chirp of the falcon feather," Slade said.

Malcom raised his brow in interest. The other falcons spoke nervously amongst each other.

"What do we do to stop this madness?" Malcom asked.

"We get the cure first. We monitor the amount that is available making sure we profit but never run the risk of becoming featherless. We control the operation," Slade explained.

"You have enough eagles to help you do that; why ask me and the rest of the falcons?" Malcom asked.

"We need more bird power behind this operation. After all, Mob Boss and his gang aren't the only obstacle we fight against. As I speak, there is a hummingbird seeking the cure," Slade said.

Malcom and the other falcons roared with laughter.

"A hummingbird? You place fear on the smallest bird species known? A hummer can't even fly too far without seeking nectar for strength," Malcom said between snorts of laughter.

Slade was annoyed at being laughed at but tried not to show his emotions. "This is no ordinary hummingbird. He has some kind of posse helping him gain this said cure. He tricked me and then escaped. With your ability to dive at speeds of two hundred miles per hour and the golden eagles' keen eyesight, we will make quite a team. Think of the profit we will make," Slade enticed.

Malcom turned to the other falcons. The greedy-eyed falcons nodded in agreement. Slade sensed victory.

"I'm Malcom falcon and you, my ally, have yourself a deal. Now where can we find this hummer?" Malcom asked.

Fun Fact: Hummingbirds have more unique flight abilities than any other bird. They are able to fly not only forward, but also backward, sideways, and straight up. They can hover extensively and can even do aerobatics such as backward somersaults.

CHAPTER SEVEN

Spa Day

Henry, Jay-Jay, Stella, and Emmett flew through a neighborhood where the houses were on cliffs with the view of the Hollywood sign. Stella glanced down and saw a huge pool and hot tub, which reminded her of her clean stone birdbath back home.

"Biggest birdbath ever!" Stella said with excitement. She flew down and Henry, Jay-Jay, and Emmett followed.

Stella tested the water with one leg, pulled her leg out, and smiled. She settled in.

Henry became anxious, "We don't have time for this, Stella."

"It's warm enough to melt butter but not hot enough to burn our toast," Stella said, relaxed.

Henry tried to relax. "Well, only for a minute. We need to keep moving."

Jay-Jay joined Stella in the water. "Get in Henry," Jay-Jay encouraged.

Henry joined his friends. They leaned back and relaxed. Emmett stayed on the rim of the hot tub, only dipping his toes in and recalling his past.

"So anyway, as I was saying earlier, my Millie loved to bake. She made pumpkin seed pie, sunflower muffins, honeysuckle pops, let's see, what else," Emmett thought a moment.

Henry had to admit even with Emmett going on and on, he felt relaxed now that the warmth of the water reached his neck. The good life didn't last long though as it was interrupted by wicked laughing. Henry, Jay-Jay, Stella, and Emmett looked at each other in confusion until they saw three young boys turn the corner. One boy was short and pudgy and wore a black T-shirt that read: "Shoot first". The other two boys were twins with bright curly red hair and freckles. They wore identical T-shirts that read: "Double Trouble".

The pudgy boy said, "My vote is to throw her in the pool!"

One of the twins cheered him on. "Yeah! See if she can swim as well as she flies."

The other twin said, "It's a hot tub, you boneheads. I say we force rotten seed in her bill again, that was funny."

"We can draw on her feathers again," the first twin suggested.

"Nah, I like the hot tub idea," the pudgy boy said.

The three boys turned the corner.

Jay-Jay's eyes widened and he said, "Uh, time to leave."

Something caught Henry's eye. "They have a bird!" Henry pointed.

The others looked closer at the boys and saw that the pudgy one held a small and frightened bright yellow canary with red, blue, and black circles drawn on her feathers with markers. She looked a bit green in the face. The boys laughed as the pudgy one threw her in the hot tub. The canary landed in the middle of the hot tub and didn't move.

"Hey, look! More birds," the pudgy boy said.

"Cool! Time for some bird soup," one of the twins said.

"No!" Henry yelled.

Henry moved forward but the twins pressed a bright red button and the hot tub turned on full blast, causing the water to circle. Henry, Jay-Jay, and Stella spun in a circle and soon the canary did also.

"Flashback of hurricane!" Jay-Jay screeched.

"Float on your back feathers," Emmett encouraged them as he flew up and out of the three evil boys' way.

Just when they thought it would never end, the hot tub came to a complete stop and the boys stopped laughing.

"Get out of my backyard this instant! I will call your parents about this!" a woman yelled.

The three boys ran off, one of them saying, "Run! It's Mrs. Taylor!"

Mrs. Taylor, a tall, thin, attractive brunette wearing pink high heels and a fancy sundress came over to the hot tub. Her small yorkie dog, who was wearing two pink bows and a fuzzy pink sweater, barked by the pool trying to get her attention. Mrs. Taylor saw the four birds looking lifeless in the hot tub. She grabbed the pool net and scooped them all out.

"Don't worry little ones, Mrs. Taylor is going to make everything better. Come Queen Elizabeth!" Mrs. Taylor said to her yorkie.

Emmett hid behind the siding of the hot tub and watched Mrs. Taylor take the birds inside her sunroom.

Slade circled above Mrs. Taylor's backyard. Malcom and the other falcons joined him. Slade landed on a palm tree and Malcom and the falcons landed nearby.

"That's them. When they come out, we will be here waiting," Slade told them.

Henry, Jay-Jay, and Stella ate from the nectar and seed that Mrs. Taylor provided. They were dry and looking better. Mrs. Taylor was hand feeding the canary and using a dropper to get water in her bill.

"I hope she will be all right," Henry said with concern.

"Me too. Those no-good sapheads ought to have their hides whipped," Stella said.

Henry nodded in agreement. "Well, let's go. We have taken a longer break than planned."

Mrs. Taylor laid the dropper to the side and placed the canary in the wide, white wire cage. She scooped Henry, Jay-Jay, and Stella up and put them in the cage too.

"Oh no! We're not staying," Stella chirped.

Mrs. Taylor did not understand Stella's chirps. She closed the cage door and headed inside her home.

Henry paced back and forth with great anxiety. "This can't be happening!" Henry felt all hope drain from his body.

A loud pecking on the glass window caught their attention. Emmett hovered outside the sun porch.

"Don't worry, old Emmett will get you out of there. I'm going to rally up some of my friends from Easy Bird Living. It may take me a few days but I'll come back for you three whippersnappers," Emmett said.

Emmett flew smack into the window. He rubbed his head.

"I'm okay. These old eyes aren't what they used to be but they still work," Emmett said still rubbing his bruised head as he flew off in a slanted pattern.

"Great! Our escape plan involves Emmett and his jolly old band of retirees," Jay-Jay said with exasperation.

Henry wasn't one to despair but he felt very discouraged by their predicament. In his mind, the wire cage was a jail that they wouldn't break free of. That night, Henry tossed and turned and when he finally fell asleep, he had a horrific nightmare. Hanna was trapped under a tree limb calling out for him. Henry woke with a jolt. He looked around and remembered his current predicament. He took a few calming breaths reminding himself it was only a dream. He told himself that in the morning he would find a way out.

The next morning, Mrs. Taylor came outside to refill the seed, water, and nectar. They all gladly ate, even the canary.

"There you go girl," Mrs. Taylor encouraged the canary.

Mrs. Taylor called for Queen Elizabeth, who was busy pawing a lizard, and she followed her inside.

Henry looked at the canary and saw that she still looked worn out. "Are you okay?" he asked.

"I will be once I find a way out of here," the canary said.

"Were you taken from your family too?" Jay-Jay asked.

"No. I'm a pet bought from the pet store. I don't remember my bird family. All I know is that I have to get as far away from humans as possible," the canary said.

"Why would you leave here? Mrs. Taylor would be a great owner," Henry said.

"Yeah, this place is a paradise for a pet bird," Stella added.

"Humans are evil. Did you not see what my owner did to me?" the canary asked.

"That was your owner?" Henry asked with shock.

"See why I won't be wearing a 'Team Human' shirt anytime soon?" the canary asked.

"But darling; not all humans are like that. Take Mrs. Taylor, for instance," Stella said.

"She is trying to gain our trust and then once she has it, *bam*! We are Queen Elizabeth's chew toys," the canary said.

"I'm nobody's chew toy," Jay-Jay said and ruffled his feathers.

"What's your name?" Henry asked.

"Sara."

"I'm Henry and this is Jay-Jay and Stella. I think I saw your picture in my book. You're a yellow canary right?"

Sara replied sarcastically, "Wow, you are really smart."

Mrs. Taylor walked back outside and Queen Elizabeth followed wagging her tail. Mrs. Taylor picked up the white wire cage and brought it with her to her pearly white BMW convertible. She placed the cage in the back seat and got on the driver's side while Queen Elizabeth jumped in the passenger seat.

A fear engulfed Henry and he wished to be back home. "Where is she bringing us?" Henry gulped.

"Where do you think? A pet store, of course. What did I tell you about humans? They can't be trusted," Sara said and sank against the wall of the cage with a sigh.

Stella became frantic. She paced the cage in a nervous way and said, "Pet store, pet store, pet store! Oh my heavens! I can't go there, it's not sanitary."

Henry realized he would need to be the calm, levelheaded one and so he said what he hoped to be the truth: "We will find a way to escape."

"Where are you from? Planet Mars? You and your friends aren't getting out of this," Sara corrected Henry.

Mrs. Taylor pulled into a shopping center and parked in front of a store called the "Fresh Market". She lifted the cage out of the back seat and Queen Elizabeth followed her dutifully. Henry watched as they passed up the door to the "Fresh Market" and headed to the corner of the shopping center, finally stopping in front of a door that read: "Pampered Pets Day Spa."

Mrs. Taylor opened the door to the day spa. Two bells chimed as the door opened and closed behind her. A young girl with curly brown hair and a splatter of freckles greeted Mrs. Taylor inside the spa. Henry could hear the tranquil sound of a water fountain and it reminded him of the stream back home.

"Welcome to Pampered Pets Day Spa. How may we pamper you?" The bubbly girl asked.

"Queen Elizabeth is ready for a shampoo and style," Mrs. Taylor responded.

Queen Elizabeth turned around in a circle for attention. Mrs. Taylor placed the white cage on the counter.

"These four could use some pampering as well. I'm going to run some errands. Call my cell when they're ready," Mrs. Taylor said patting Queen Elizabeth on the head before she exited the spa.

The young girl picked the cage up with Henry, Jay-Jay, Stella, and Sara and walked toward the spa relaxation area. Queen Elizabeth followed behind, wagging her tail. Relaxing music filled the air, the smell of cucumbers drifted across their beaks, the sound of flowing fountains could be heard, and soft candlelight lit the dark hallways. Henry caught a glimpse of himself in a mirror and was surprised to see he was smiling despite everything. He looked a mess of matted feathers but smiling he was.

Ten minutes later, Henry was being fed trumpet vines; Jay-Jay enjoyed a massage by a woman with tiny hands and fingers; Stella, to her utmost joy, was covered in soap and bubbles and relaxing in a birdbath for one. Sara's red, blue, and black circles were gone and the staff cleaned one of her many cuts. Sara winced as she felt the sting from the saturated cotton ball and looked at the humans with a mixture of fear and disgust. Queen Elizabeth's fur was being blown dry.

An hour later, Henry was getting a much-needed shoulder rub while his top feathers were being brushed. He was also still being hand-fed trumpet vines. Jay-Jay had small cucumbers on his eyes and was sound asleep, his head hanging off a bird hammock. Stella was perched on a small bird swing as a staff member painted her toes bright pink. Sara was being slathered with an ointment to prevent infection. She looked a little worried but, as the staff member began to massage the ointment in a gentle way, Sara began to relax. Queen Elizabeth chewed on a huge bone, while a staff member combed her fur.

A few hours after that, a staff member fanned Henry as he ate yet another trumpet vine. Henry now wore a small green bow tie around his neck. Jay-Jay was still sound asleep and snoring, his head still hanging off the side of the hammock. Jay-Jay had no idea there was a huge blue bow tied around his neck and Henry found that quite humorous. Stella had a bright pink bow around her neck; she was wide awake and very happy to be clean again. Stella proudly relaxed in the pink fluffy bird bed the staff provided. Even Sara looked healthy and happy. Her feathers shimmered. She wore a purple bow around her neck and had purple toes to match. Queen Elizabeth had two red bows on each side of her ears and one red bow fashioned at the top of her wagging tail.

Henry was so full; he couldn't eat another bite. He decided to save the last trumpet vine. He opened his backpack and placed the trumpet vine inside. The list for the cure fell out and Henry studied it. His eyes widened in realization. Lavender! Lavender oil was on the list. "Spas had lavender oil," Henry thought as he stuffed the list back into his backpack. He needed to find the lavender oil and fast.

Henry flew upward. One of the girls on staff giggled and reached for him.

"Oh no, little one. Come back down," Spa girl corrected Henry.

She reached for Henry again but he dove down and away from her and headed toward the back of the spa. Henry eyed the cabinets quickly. There were dozens upon dozens of essential oils. His heart pounded. "Lavender oil, where are you?" Henry thought as he continued to scan the shelves.

Henry heard the spa girl call for help and he knew he was running out of time. He flew down to the bottom shelf and began to read each label: "Grapefruit, vanilla, tea tree, peppermint, lemon. Come on, come on," Henry said frustrated.

The spa girl walked into the room and spotted Henry. Henry turned back to the oils. He saw eucalyptus, orange, until finally – *Lavender*! Henry grabbed the lavender oil and stuffed it into his backpack. He zipped it up before spa girl grabbed him and took him back to the front.

"Don't worry, little fellow, Mrs. Taylor is on her way," the spa girl said.

Finally, the day of relaxation ended and they were back in Mrs. Taylor's car. Henry and Stella watched the sights of California zoom by as Mrs. Taylor moved in and out of traffic. Sara stared at Mrs. Taylor as though trying to figure the woman out. Queen Elizabeth perched her front paws on the rim of the open window, her red-bowed ears flapping in the wind. Jay-Jay was still sound asleep and snoring loudly.

Fun Fact: Canaries are great singers and naturally friendly, which are the very reasons they make popular pets.

CHAPTER EIGHT

Sara's Sweet Song

Slade, Malcom, and the falcons followed Mrs. Taylor's car discreetly.

"What do you think is going on?" Malcom asked.

"I have no idea. They went into that building and came out looking refreshed and wearing those ridiculous bows," Slade answered.

"Do you think the human is helping them?" Malcom asked.

"I wouldn't put anything passed these three. It doesn't matter though. We will wait and if she doesn't set them free, we will break them out ourselves. That cure is mine!"

"Ours," Malcom corrected.

Later that night, Mrs. Taylor brought fresh birdseed and cold water to the birds. She even added a few colorful plants in the cage as well as a brightly colored wooden perch. Sara seemed to perk up at the sight of them.

Jay-Jay woke up and stretched. Everyone was eating. Henry and Stella exchanged amused glances as they anticipated Jay-Jay's reaction to wearing a bow. Jay-Jay joined them. As he approached the seed, he caught his reflection in the small, oval bird mirror.

"Aaahhh! What is the meaning of this?" Jay-Jay screeched as he tried to tug the blue ribbon off his neck.

Sara giggled.

"It's only a dream. Sara laughed; Sara doesn't laugh," Jay-Jay said.

"I laugh. Sometimes," Sara said.

Mrs. Taylor walked into the sun porch and refilled the water.

"Sing a sweet song for me, pretty one," Mrs. Taylor addressed the bird.

Stella tweeted softly and then stopped when she realized she was the only one tweeting. Mrs. Taylor smiled at Stella and walked back inside.

"Ah Stella, hate to burst your bubble but she was talking to me. I didn't want to upstage anyone, you know with being this handsome and then a great singing voice to boot," Jay-Jay said proudly.

"She was talking to me. Canaries are known for their sweet singing voice but I will never sing for a human. I decided against that career a long time ago," Sara told them.

"Sara, you should give Mrs. Taylor a chance. Can't you see how much she loves you?" Henry asked.

Sara turned her back on Henry. Henry felt sorry for Sara. She had never felt the love of family.

"So, how do we escape?" Jay-Jay asked still tugging on his bow.

"I thought you said this place is perfect?" Sara accused.

"We need to get back home and make sure our families are okay and let them see we aren't dead," Henry explained.

"Dead?" Sara questioned.

"We traveled here due to a hurricane and the damage back home is horrible. We don't know who's left," Henry explained.

Jay-Jay continued to tug on his bow. He tugged so hard, he fell into Sara and Henry.

"Okay, will somebody help me?" Jay-Jay asked.

"Goodness gracious! It looks good on you. Keep it," Stella told Jay-Jay.

The next morning, Mrs. Taylor walked into the sun porch and picked up their cage. She opened the porch door, wiped away tears, and opened the cage door.

"Okay you guys, go show those other birds who's boss. With these new looks, you all will be the best looking birds in town," Mrs. Taylor said.

Henry felt a surge of joy. Stella and Jay-Jay exchanged happy glances. Sara listened in shock.

"She's letting us go," Henry said with excitement.

"Well salt my stick. She sure is," Stella exclaimed.

They all flew out except for Sara. Henry hovered near the cage. Jay-Jay and Stella landed on a nearby branch.

"Are you coming, Sara?" Henry asked.

Mrs. Taylor said to Sara: "Oh please tell me you want to stay. I would love to have you. Pampered Pets Day Spa would be a weekly treat."

Sara looked from Mrs. Taylor to Henry. "She's better than my last owner," Sara said and smiled.

Henry smiled back. Sara had found a family after all. Mrs. Taylor closed the cage door. As Henry, Jay-Jay, and Stella flew away, they heard the sweet song of Sara, the yellow canary, singing for Mrs. Taylor at last.

Meanwhile, Slade, Malcom, and the falcons slept soundly. Sara's singing woke Slade. Slade took a moment to adjust his eyes to the light. He saw Mrs. Taylor walking toward her sun porch. He looked closer and saw that Sara was the only one left in the cage.

Slade whacked Malcom on the head. "Get up you fools! ! They're gone! We have to find them."

Fun Fact: The golden eagle is North America's largest bird of prey. It can grow to a length of three feet, with a wingspan of six to seven feet.

CHAPTER NINE

Who is the Leader?

Henry, Jay-Jay, and Stella had made progress in their flight to get back home. Of course, Henry still had items to collect so he would need to sidetrack Jay-Jay and Stella at certain points in the trip. He found it harder and harder to keep his sister's secret. It was there on the tip of his tongue. If he told them, maybe they would have ideas on where to find the items. But then again, one particular item on the list could have them flying for the hills. No, it was best he kept this to himself.

They now soared over desert sands with cactus plants below. As they flew down to rest, Jay-Jay landed on a cactus and screeched in pain, rubbing his bottom.

"For the record, I do *not* like cactus," Jay-Jay informed them while pulling out cactus prickles from his bottom tail feathers.

"Don't land smack dab in the middle of them and you won't have a problem, sugar," Stella teased.

Jay-Jay gave Stella a "that's obvious" look and said, "Don't call me sugar." He pulled the last cactus prickle from his tail feathers and tossed it on the ground. Henry grabbed the cactus prickle and stuffed it into his backpack. Henry crossed off cactus prickle from the cure list.

Jay-Jay and Stella exchanged confused glances.

"Really? A cactus prickle from my butt? I'm sure there's something better than that to remember this dry place. Let's see, there's . . . " Jay-Jay stopped talking. He saw something in between the cactus. He moved to get a better look. It was a nest among the cactus with a bird sleeping inside.

"Who's that?" Jay-Jay asked.

A cactus wren with spotted tail feathers slept soundly in her nest. Henry, Jay-Jay, and Stella moved in toward her to get a better look.

"It's late to still be asleep. This bird must be worn slap out or lazy," Stella whispered.

Hearing voices, the wren slowly sat up. She stretched her wings and stared at her intruders in irritation.

"Can you be quiet? I was having a wonderful dream. I was about to find the worm!" she told them.

"The early bird gets the worm . . . not the bird that sleeps and dreams about it!" Jay-Jay said.

The wren ignored Jay-Jay's teasing. She jumped out of her nest and walked past Henry, Jay-Jay, and Stella. Using her beak, she started to move loose leaves and ground litter around in a frenzy.

Stella looked on with concern. "Now you're in a tizzy to find food? I'm sure there are still some worms around."

"I'm not in a tizzy! I'm simply doing what I do every day. I sleep late and then search for food before making a couple more nests to spread around the desert," the wren corrected Stella.

Stella glanced in the nest. "This nest seems good enough to me. Although there are a few needles askew here." Stella pressed her wings against the loose needles in an attempt to put them neatly in place.

The wren shooed Stella away from her nest. She was offended by the lack of privacy.

"It was very good until *you* came along! Now I have to make a new nest and some decoys," the wren said, still irritated.

Henry was intrigued. "What's your name? I'm Henry Humming."

"Catie. I'm a cactus wren bird. That's why I sleep late; it's in my nature. Now if you will excuse me, I have a worm to find and nests to build."

"Wait! How far are we from Louisiana?" Henry asked.

"Far enough. Keep flying east. Why are you going there anyhow? If you are migrating for the winter you could stay here in this desert. The nights are cool but the days are warm," Catie told Henry.

"Thank you, but we have to get back home. We have already lost enough time," Henry replied.

"Suit yourself. Now if you will excuse me," Catie said and flew away.

"Strange little bird," Jay-Jay said looking in her nest with a shrug.

"I like her. I think she wanted us to stay and keep her company. She must be lonely but will not admit it." Henry jotted her name down in his journal.

"She said to fly east but we live in southern Louisiana. I think we better fly south," Jay-Jay said.

Henry put his journal back in his backpack. "We do live in southern Louisiana but we need to fly east."

"How would you know? You have never flown this far before," Jay-Jay told Henry.

"Neither have you. Why must you argue with every decision I make? I've gotten us this far haven't I?" Henry asked.

"This *far*? So far we have picked up some strange souvenirs, we were almost eaten by an eagle, spun around in a huge birdbath by demon children, and then trapped in a wire cage. What's next?" Jay-Jay asked Henry.

"Y'all, let's look at the compass," Stella interrupted.

"I didn't want to say anything, but I should be the leader. You're too emotional over what may or may not have happened to Hanna," Jay-Jay told Henry.

Those words made Henry irate. "That's why *I* should be the leader. If you lead, there will be no purpose other than how many times we stop to groom ourselves!"

Stella looked from Henry to Jay-Jay. She tried to get their attention again and said, "Remember to load your brain before you two shoot your beaks off."

Jay-Jay paid no attention to Stella and continued to argue his point. "At least I'm not calling myself a big brother when in fact you are not!" Jay-Jay yelled.

"What's that supposed to mean?" Henry shouted.

"Oh, come on, your egg cracked one day before Hanna's. Big tweeting deal!" Jay-Jay said.

Stella tried again. "Oh my stars, y'all stop before there's any hurt feelings and bruised egos."

Henry pressed on. "Hanna may only be one day younger but her handicap keeps her in danger, so I stepped up to be the big brother and protect her."

Jay-Jay threw his wings up in annoyance, "Protect her from what? The other backyard birds we've known for years? The old couple that fall asleep on the porch swing for hours at a time?" Jay-Jay asked sarcastically.

"You know very well we have to help her to the birdbath and feeders. Plus, there's more than that. You don't understand," Henry said. Henry felt an immense surge of anger and hurt. He wondered how Jay-Jay could be so selfish?

"Did you ever think that perhaps, just maybe, if you and your parents would let her practice flying, that she could fend for herself! Y'all smother her!" Jay-Jay retaliated.

Stella spoke, "Jay-Jay! Quit being ugly. If you two don't stop, we won't get home. Stop fighting and take the compass out."

"We do not smother Hanna!" Henry told Jay-Jay.

"It's true. Every bird knows it. They tweet behind your backs." Jay-Jay mimicked the birds: "Those Hummings are so overprotective, so overbearing. How sad for poor Hanna. She will never learn to live on her own."

Henry fumed in anger and before he could stop himself, he blurted out, "Hanna has the bird disease!"

Stella gasped. Jay-Jay rolled his eyes in disbelief.

"Now you're making up lies to make me feel bad," Jay-Jay accused.

"How dare you call me a liar, Jay-Jay. If you know so much more, then find your own way home," Henry told him.

"I will! A jay doesn't need to take directions from a tiny hummer," Jay-Jay said.

Stella moved next to Henry. "Um, I think we best stick together. Especially since we heard the eagle, Slade, a few nights ago."

Jay-Jay ignored Stella and flew off.

"Let him go," Henry told Stella. He knew Stella was right but he was hurt and angry. He didn't want to see Jay-Jay ever again or at least that's how he felt in that moment.

"I don't know, Henry. It isn't safe for Jay-Jay to be on his own. I say we go get him and you two talk it over," Stella encouraged.

Henry shook his head, "No way! Not after what he said. He thinks he is so big and bad, well let's see who gets home first."

"Henry, is it true about Hanna?" Stella asked.

Henry nodded. Stella grabbed him in a hug. Henry was relieved now that Stella knew. He was tired of hiding such a huge secret from his friend.

"Why didn't you tell us?" Stella asked.

"Hanna wanted to but my parents and I thought it best to handle it on our own. I guess I thought what good would it do?"

Stella pulled away from Henry with an offended look. "What good would it do? We could have helped, provided moral support, took turns caring for her, had a fundraiser, and don't forget about my sweet tea that cures even the saddest heart. All this time, I thought you were being overprotective because of her one wing but it was because she was sick. Why can't you see that family isn't just blood? I'm your family too, Henry."

Henry felt a heat spread over his entire body. He looked down in shame. Stella was right. Why did he try to do this all on his own?

"Now you hate me too," Henry said to Stella.

"Heavens no. I'm just hurt, that's all. But I forgive you and I want to help you," Stella said and patted Henry reassuringly. "We will figure something out."

Henry stepped back and wiped his tears. "That's what I've been doing."

Henry pulled his backpack from over his shoulders and grabbed the list of the cure and handed it over to Stella. Stella looked over the list and back at Henry.

"Those weren't just souvenirs, were they?" Stella asked.

Henry gently took the list back and put it in his backpack for safekeeping. "No. Hanna doesn't have much time."

"What's next on the list?" Stella asked.

"A special nectar from a rare flower. I'm not sure where to find it but I have to get my feathers on it," Henry explained.

"That one doesn't worry my mind as much as the last ingredient on that list," Stella said. "But don't you fret. It will all come out in the wash."

Henry smiled despite himself. Stella's southern sayings seemed to become more prominent when she was worried or angry. He was glad to have her on his side. She was a true friend and somehow, despite the fact that the remaining items seemed impossible, Stella had a way of making it all seem okay.

Fun Fact: Finches prefer the company of other finches and birds to that of a human companion.

CHAPTER TEN

Jake the Blue Jay

The desert offered a warm quiet that would make most birds relax but Jay-Jay preferred noise. He wondered if he was capable of making it home alone with only himself to talk to. He quickly shook the doubt from his mind. What was he thinking? Of course he could. He was a jay and jays could do anything and needed no one to help.

Jay-Jay flew over the cactus making sure to keep his flight at a height that wouldn't threaten his tail feathers. He was pleased when he saw a lone tree up in the distance; a very nice change from the cactus. He landed on the branch and enjoyed the shade.

"I don't need Henry or any bird for that matter," Jay-Jay mumbled to himself.

Jay-Jay was startled when a flash of blue flew around the tree and landed next to him. With everything that had happened thus far, Jay-Jay held his wings up, ready to fight, but he lowered them when he saw the older blue jay staring back at him in surprise.

"Haven't seen another jay around these parts in quite some time. Name's Jake," Jake Jay said holding his wing out to Jay-Jay.

Jay-Jay hesitated a moment but eventually shook Jake's wing, "My name is Jay-Jay."

"Nice to meet you. Where you heading?" Jake asked.

"Louisiana and I'm going my own way," Jay-Jay grumbled.

"I see," Jake said, a bit amused.

Jay-Jay could tell Jake was waiting for an explanation and he was glad to get it off of his chest. "I was traveling with Henry and Stella, my ex friends, but I don't need them anymore," Jay-Jay said stubbornly.

"Ah, they aren't jays are they?" Jake asked.

Jay-Jay huffed. "Not even close. A hummer and a yellow finch. They don't compare to my size, smarts, and beauty."

Jake smiled. "You are a fine looking jay."

"Thanks. You're not too bad yourself for an older jay," Jay-Jay said.

Jake roared in laughter. "I still have some charm left in these old feathers. I only wish I hadn't been so vain in the past."

"Why?" Jay-Jay asked.

"It's one thing to have confidence and another to be vain. Look around, Jay-Jay. I live all alone. I have done so for many years."

"A handsome jay like you?" Jay-Jay asked puzzled.

"Looks fade and it's what's inside that really counts anyhow," Jake said.

"So you've never had a wife or children? What about your friends? Where did they all go?" Jay-Jay asked.

Jake looked down in sorrow. "Let me tell you a little story, Jay-Jay."

Jay-Jay settled down on the branch to listen. Jake began telling his story and Jay-Jay imagined he was there watching as a younger version of Jake flew around the park, racing around each tree trunk until landing on a stone birdbath.

~~ Flashback ~~

Two cardinals, Alyssa and Andrew, flew around the same trees and landed next to Jake. They were out of breath, gasping for air and holding their sides.

"Beat you two again! You two don't even give me a challenge," young Jake told them.

"Show off," Andrew said in anger.

Alyssa caught her breath and spoke, "Andrew's right; you brag too much."

Jake shook his head with a smile. "I don't have to brag. My record speaks for itself."

Alyssa and Andrew rolled their eyes. Jake began splashing in the birdbath, soaking them with the water.

"Hey, watch it," Alyssa said.

Before Jake could reply, a beautiful blue jay landed on the stone birdbath. Jake's beak dropped open in awe. "Who . . . who are you?"

The beautiful female blue jay spoke in a very proper lady-like voice. "I'm Maggie Josephine Jay."

Jake lifted his dripping wet wing out of the birdbath and offered it to Maggie. "I'm Jake."

Maggie shook Jake's wing happily. "Nice to make your acquaintance. I'm new here and was wondering if one of you would mind showing me around?"

Jake pushed through the birdbath, splashing everyone, and landed next to Maggie. "I will," he said eagerly.

"Oh how lovely of you, Jake," Maggie said with a sweet smile.

Jake paused in his storytelling and Jay-Jay shook his head trying to come back out of the fog of the story. Jay-Jay looked at the older Jake.

"What happened next?" Jay-Jay asked.

"She was my dream bird. I couldn't take my eyes off of her," Jake told him.

"But where is she now?" Jay-Jay asked.

"Wait and listen. You will see," Jake continued with his story and Jay-Jay felt he was there again, watching a young Jake fly around the park with Maggie.

~~Flashback~~

A human husband and wife sat on a park bench tossing breadcrumbs toward some ducks. Young Jake brought Maggie to where they sat.

"Let's see who can get the most crumbs," young Jake said to Maggie.

Jake flew toward the crumbs and stuffed his beak. Maggie, who stayed on the bench, giggled when she saw Jake's cheeks so full of crumbs that some spilled out of his mouth. Jake swallowed and smiled.

"I won but don't worry; you will get the hang of it. Come on, I'll show you my nest," young Jake told Maggie.

Maggie followed young Jake to his nest. His nest was large enough for an eagle, which led Maggie to believe he had quite a large family. However, when she glanced around the nest, there were several picture frames but the pictures were all of Jake. Maggie studied each photo in a bit of confusion.

"Don't you have any pictures of family and friends?" she asked.

"Nah, I wanted my nest to look good. I got all the good looks in the family and none of my friends are as handsome as me," Jake told her.

Maggie was shocked. "What if I gave you a photo of myself? Where would you put it?"

"You're a beauty but there's really no more room in my nest," young Jake responded.

Maggie was so hurt by Jake's words that she blurted out, "Then let me make room," and with that said, she flew out and away from Jake and his nest.

Jay-Jay looked at Jake, who was looking down in shame but managed to continue speaking, "I saw her around the park and tried to show off for her but nothing worked. A few years later, she married Andrew. At the time, I thought, a cardinal! Is she out of her feathers?" Jake said.

"She had to be out of her feathers. You dodged a bullet," Jay-Jay said.

"No, Andrew was a fine bird. She chose right," Jake corrected him.

Jay-Jay raised his brows, "How can you say that?"

"After Maggie married Andrew, I realized I had no one. My family migrated and never returned, I had no friends, and the love of my life married another," Jake said. "My vanity and self-centered attitude cost me everything. I left the park and came here to the desert."

"That's a sad story," Jay-Jay said.

Jake nodded in agreement. "You should find your friends Jay-Jay. Family and friends are so important."

Jay-Jay wasn't so sure. "What about you?"

"It is high time I take my own advice. It's never too late to make friends. I made one in you. I'm going back home and make peace with everyone. A new start!" Jake said.

Jay-Jay pondered this. He imagined living a life of solitude like Jake had for so many years only to realize in the end that family and friends matter. Jay-Jay couldn't let his ego keep him from doing what was right. He loved his family and friends. He couldn't fly away when things didn't go his way. That was selfish of him and he knew that now thanks to Jake.

"Well, which way are you going to fly?" Jake asked.

"Toward my friends," Jay-Jay said. "I owe them an apology. Thank you Jake and good luck to you. You deserve to be happy too."

Jake smiled. "That's the spirit. Good luck to you too Jay-Jay and thank you. If I hadn't heard my own advice out loud, I may have never realized what I have been missing."

Jay-Jay winked. "It was nice to meet you."

Jake smiled as Jay-Jay flew off to find Henry and Stella. Jay-Jay wondered if Henry would forgive him. He wondered how mad Stella would be. Several thoughts of doubt began to flood Jay-Jay's head and he needed a minute to think of an apology. He flew down and landed on the desert sands. And for once, he welcomed the warm quiet as it allowed him to think.

Fun Fact: The blue jay has been chosen as mascots of various sports groups. One example is Canada's professional baseball team, the Toronto Blue Jays.

CHAPTER ELEVEN

Team Work

Slade, Malcom, and the other falcons flew above the desert while Henry and Stella stood below pondering their next move and how to find the nectar. Slade and Malcom landed next to one of Catie's nests.

Slade noticed three different bird tracks in the sand. He nudged Malcom and pointed with an evil grin.

"They're close," Slade said to Malcom.

The other falcons laughed in triumph.

Jay-Jay stood on the other side of the large cactus that Slade landed near. Jay-Jay was deep in thought, practicing his apology when he heard the laughter. He tiptoed closer and positioned himself carefully behind the largest cactus arm. He peered between the prickle and saw Slade, Malcom, and the rest of the falcons.

"By now, the hummer may have all the ingredients for the cure," Malcom said.

"I'm positive he doesn't. We will stop him before he does. I say we take what he has of the cure and get the answers to what's left," Slade said.

Malcom nodded. The other falcons cheered him on.

"Yes, have him make the cure for us!" Malcom added.

Slade shook his head. "Once we have the ingredient list, there's no need to keep him or his posse alive."

Malcom looked shocked. "We kill them?"

Slade nodded. "Eat them; kill them, all I know is the hummer is mine."

Malcom agreed. "Very well. Let's go!"

"Yeah, let's get them!" the other falcons cheered.

They all flew up in the air with confidence and a killing gleam in their eyes.

Jay-Jay, who heard every word, was shocked. "So that was why Henry was being so weird… he's searching for the bird cure. He was telling the truth about Hanna," Jay-Jay whispered to himself. He had to save his friends. But how? Just then, he noted the size of the cactus prickle in front of him. His bottom was still sore and this gave him a great idea. Jay-Jay started to work the prickles off the cactus. Nobody was going to hurt his best friends, not if he could help it.

Jay-Jay flew as fast as he could. He saw Henry and Stella from a distance. But he also saw Slade, Malcom, and the falcons trailing behind them from above. Jay-Jay did what he did best.

"*Screech! Screech! Screech*!" Jay-Jay gave the warning call.

Henry and Stella turned around in time to see Slade, Malcom, and the falcons tailing them. Slade gave Henry his most wicked smile and circled around him and Stella, forcing them down to the desert sand.

Slade landed in front of them while Malcom and the other falcons surrounded them.

"Slade caught up to you, Hummer. You owe me a dinner and dessert. There's also the small matter of a cure I'd like to get my wings on," Slade said.

Henry clutched his backpack protectively. Jay-Jay flew low and readied his cactus prickles flying full speed toward Slade.

"No one messes with my friends," Jay-Jay said flying straight into Slade's rear-end tail feathers.

Slade was so focused on Henry and Stella it was too late to move out of Jay-Jay's way. The cactus prickles pierced his bottom and he flew up with a screech holding his rear end. Malcom flew toward Jay-Jay. Henry and Stella started grabbing as many cactus prickles as they could.

"Jay-Jay! Catch!" Henry tossed the cactus prickles to his friend.

Jay-Jay caught the prickles and held one in each wing; he pointed them toward Malcom. Henry and Stella steadied their own prickles, ready to battle the villains.

"No one needs to get hurt. We only ask for what you have of the cure and the list," Malcom lied.

"Liar! I heard everything, and you plan to take the cure and then kill us," Jay-Jay said.

"Kill us! Well, aren't you a little ray of pitch black," Stella said.

Henry, Stella, and Jay-Jay moved closer together as Slade and the falcons joined Malcom and formed a circle around the trio. Henry gripped the cactus prickles and with all his might, he threw one of the prickles at Malcom's wing. Malcom cringed in pain as he looked down at the prickle piercing his right wing. Malcom used his beak to pull the prickle out and spit it out on the ground in front of Henry.

"I'll get you for that!" Malcom moved with purpose toward Henry.

But Slade flew into Malcom knocking him to the ground with a screech. "He's mine, Malcom."

"Get him off of me," Malcom ordered his falcon followers.

The falcons rushed to pull Slade off of Malcom. Henry, Jay-Jay, and Stella took advantage of the moment and flew off as fast as they could.

Catie, who had been napping in her nest, looked up and saw Henry, Jay-Jay, and Stella panicking. "Down here," Catie called to them.

The three birds dove toward Catie.

"We're being followed," Henry blurted.

Catie lifted one of her decoy nests to reveal a small but deep hole. "Quick, under here."

Henry, Jay-Jay, and Stella jumped inside. Catie dropped the nest back on top of the hole and got inside. Seconds later, Slade, Malcom, and the falcons flew down by Catie's nest. Catie pretended to be startled awake.

"Excuse me. I'm trying to sleep," Catie said matter of fact.

Slade and Malcom exchanged curious glances.

"My apologies, cactus wren. We are in search of three birds that have committed a horrible crime. One's a hummer. Have you seen them?" Slade asked.

Under Catie's nest, in the dark hole, Henry, Jay-Jay, and Stella clutched onto each other and exchanged fearful glances. Back above, Catie remained surprisingly calm.

"I would never associate with jailbirds," Catie replied.

"But how would you know they were jailbirds unless they told you?" Slade interrogated her.

"I'm not one to socialize. As it is, you are the first bird I've spoken to all day. I have not seen any other birds. I suggest you be on your way as I have other decoy nests to make now that you've found mine," Catie replied.

Slade studied Catie's face for any signs of lying. Malcom became impatient.

"We're wasting time! Let's go," Malcom said with irritation.

Slade agreed. "Very well, but should I find out you're lying, you will need much more than decoy nests to escape me. Good day, wren," Slade said before flying off.

Malcom and the falcons followed Slade. Catie watched until they flew out of sight, and then she jumped out of her nest and lifted it.

"It's safe now. You can come out," Catie told them.

Henry, Jay-Jay, and Stella slowly emerged from the hole. Catie moved the nest back.

"I'm not even going to ask how three birds like you managed to anger a golden eagle and a group of mean falcons, but I suggest you watch your backs on the journey home," Catie advised.

Henry hugged Catie. He was so grateful for her help. "Catie, thank you. You may have very well saved our lives."

Catie gently removed Henry. "Don't mention it. Now if you will excuse me, I have my work cut out for me today. I need a new nest and a new hole," Catie said with a smile before flying off and away.

Jay-Jay turned to Henry. "I'm so sorry about what I said earlier. Especially about calling you a liar. I'll do anything to help Hanna," Jay-Jay said.

Henry patted Jay-Jay's shoulder. "Don't worry about that, Jay-Jay. Thank you for saving us back there."

"It was nothing. I couldn't have found the strength to be so brave if it weren't for the fear of losing my best friends," Jay-Jay said.

"This calls for a group hug y'all." Stella pulled Henry and Jay-Jay into her wings.

Henry felt a surge of hope now that Jay-Jay was back with them. He had no resentment toward his friend. His heart was full of love.

"Now let's get out of here before Slade and his bandwagon of falcon freaks come back!" Jay-Jay said.

Fun Fact: Falcons have a unique hunting technique. They dive at their prey and catch it in midair, taking them by surprise.

CHAPTER TWELVE

The Seed Money

The three small birds arrived at the Grand Canyon in Arizona. The Grand Canyon overwhelmed them with its size. It was enormous and they looked like tiny specks of dust in comparison to the sharp rocky cliffs that surrounded them on every side. They listened carefully to the rustling winds of the canyon and the rush of nearby water.

Henry felt blessed to have come this far, to see such beauty. He wanted to remember this moment, take in every detail, and share it with Hanna.

"How lovely! That water below looks so clean. I have to bathe in there," Stella said with excitement.

"It really is beautiful," Jay-Jay chimed.

"Yes," Henry said, and took a deep breath.

They grabbed each other's wings and landed on a nearby Arizona walnut tree overlooking a field of sparse yellow grass and a few shrubs of cactus. The looming rocks surrounded them; the view was breathtaking.

Stella looked skyward and saw a huge bird. "Goodness gracious; what's that?"

Henry looked up, "Oh no . . . *hide*!"

Henry flew into the bulk of the Arizona walnut tree, taking cover in the green leaves. Jay-Jay and Stella stayed frozen in place looking at Henry with confusion.

"Hide? Why are we hiding from that big bird after we have already met a bigger bird than that one?" Jay-Jay questioned.

"*The Seeds of Life* describes that bird as violent," Henry told them.

"Henry, you can't believe everything you read in a book," Stella lectured.

Jay-Jay put his wings up in a punching manner as though he was about to box the bird. "What kind of bird is it, Henry?" Jay-Jay asked, continuing his practice swings.

"That bird is a California condor, a vulture," Henry replied.

Something about the sound of that didn't sit well with Stella. She scooted under the Arizona walnut tree with Henry.

"What is a vulture?" Stella asked fearfully.

Now even Jay-Jay was seeking cover under the leaves next to them.

"Well, in *The Seeds of Life* it says a vulture is a large bird that lives in the Grand Canyon and can eat deer and cow," Henry explained.

"A deer? A cow?" Jay-Jay screeched.

"Shhh! The vulture might hear you!" Stella scolded.

Henry looked skyward and gulped. "Too late!"

Jay-Jay and Stella followed his gaze and saw that the vulture was heading straight for them. They all pressed together in fear. Henry opened his beak to say something but before he could speak the huge vulture landed on the same branch as them.

Snap! The branch snapped and they went flying in different directions only to land in the field below.

The vulture, who wore a colorful sombrero on his head, spoke to Henry, Jay-Jay, and Stella with a Mexican accent. "Who are jou guys?"

Jay-Jay ran behind Henry, pushing Henry forward to answer. Stella stayed behind Jay-Jay, shaking in fear.

Henry raised his voice to answer. "We do not taste good at all."

"I don't care how jou taste my amigos. I just asked jou guys what jour names are," the vulture said.

Jay-Jay whispered to Henry and Stella, "Did you hear that? He doesn't care how we taste! He'll swallow us whole!" Jay-Jay started to panic.

Henry spoke louder hoping to attract attention. "Does it matter? Are you going to tell the world you ate me, Henry Robert Humming?"

"Why are jou shouting Henry Robert Humming? Know what? Can I just call jou Henry? I don't like long names," the vulture asked.

Henry gulped and said, "I guess."

The vulture looked straight at Stella. "Jou, very pretty bird, what's jour name?"

Jay-Jay stepped forward and said, "Jay-Jay is my name and I do not taste good. I'm really gross. Downright nasty. Back home they call me poo stank."

"Not jou!" The vulture pointed to Stella. "Her."

"Stella, and I'm not as sweet as a peach."

"Jou guys sure do care a lot about how jou might taste. I am Victor Aaron Ambrosio Berto Cruz Diego Domingo Enrique Garcia Hector Vulture," the vulture told them.

Henry, Jay-Jay, and Stella's beaks dropped open in shock. Henry couldn't imagine having such a long name.

The vulture frowned. "That's right. Go ahead and laugh if jou want to. I don't know why I bother to tell anyone my real name. It's too hard to remember, anyhow. Just call me Vinnie."

Jay-Jay asked, "Vinnie, how long do we have before you eat us? I don't mind small talk but I think it's making me more nervous not knowing when it will happen."

"Eat jou?" Vinnie laughed loudly. "Now why would I go and do a thing like that? Jou guys are kind of loco. I was worried jou guys would make fun of my long name and instead jou are the ones with the problem. Thinking me, lovable Vinnie, would want to eat jou guys!" Vinnie slapped his wing against his stomach and roared with laughter, holding his side and tumbling down on the ground.

Henry, Jay-Jay, and Stella relaxed.

"So you don't want to eat us?" Stella asked.

"Are you dead?" Vinnie asked.

"Uh, no," Stella responded.

"Then no, I don't want to eat jou. I only eat dead animals. Gosh, jou guys must have thought I was really gross, going around eating animals that are alive!" Vinnie laughed again.

Henry, Jay-Jay, and Stella looked at Vinnie curiously.

"Jou three are funny. I think I like jou. Look, I tend to like dead deer and cows only, so why don't jou rest easy and enjoy the view of my home. The humans sure do," Vinnie said, waving a wing to indicate the view and the humans.

A lady tour guide gave a tour to families down below. A few "oohs" and "aahs" could be heard coming from the tourists.

"Did jou guys see everything?" Vinnie asked.

"Not everything," Henry answered.

Vinnie smiled and motioned for them to follow him. They all took flight and toured the Grand Canyon with Vinnie as their tour guide. They flew over some Pinyon Pine, Gambel Oak, and Utah Juniper. They saw sheep, bobcats, mule deer, and rock squirrels during their tour. The Colorado River expanded below them and glistened in the sun. Henry, Jay-Jay, and Stella smiled. Henry knew they'd remember this forever.

They gazed down at the Hoover Dam and the many stunning colors of the landscape that stained the rock walls of the Grand Canyon. When they were done touring, they landed on a pine tree on the Grand Canyon edge. It was one of the best views they had seen. Another vulture joined them. She wore a single red camellia flower in her feathers.

"This is my little sister, Victoria Alma Angela Blanca Cruza Dina Dolores Enriqua Guadalupe Heidi Vulture," Vinnie said, introducing his sister.

Vinnie's sister smiled and said, "You can call me Victoria."

"Good enough," Jay-Jay said.

Henry and Stella smirked and shrugged. Henry felt at peace. He wasn't sure how long it would last but he soaked it in. He knew Hanna would want him to.

The moon came up and darkness fell over the Grand Canyon. Henry, Jay-Jay, Stella, Vinnie, and Victoria flew down from the branch and landed on the ground. Five other vultures were there, waiting for them. One of the vultures was taller than the rest, with a jagged scar above his eyebrow and another on his wing. He stood in the front with two rounder vultures slightly behind him on each side. Two muscular vultures stood in the very back with mean looks in their eyes.

"How many family members do you have?" Jay-Jay asked Vinnie and Victoria.

"That's not our family," Vinnie said.

The tall vulture with the jagged scar spoke with an Italian accent, "Where's the seed money?"

"The what?" Vinnie asked.

"What's he talking about?" Henry asked.

"I'm the boss, so don't play dumb. That's how a bird gets killed around here. Capiche?" Boss said.

The four other vultures laughed wickedly and pulled out sticks that had been sharpened on the end to look like daggers.

Henry looked at Vinnie for answers. "Vinnie?"

"I assure jou Amigo, we don't have no seed money," Vinnie told Boss.

"Wrong answer! Who's your godfather?" Boss asked.

"Oh he passed away years ago. If he owed jou any seed money, jou won't be seeing it," Vinnie said.

Henry glanced over Boss and his gang. An extreme uneasiness filled his body. He wondered if they could outfly them.

"Then it looks like you're going to have to pay his debts because as Godfather of New York, I didn't travel all this way to not get paid!" Boss said.

His posse stepped forward with their sharpened sticks raised.

Henry chimed in. "We will help you look for the seed money, Vinnie."

Boss looked at the vulture on his right and then the one on his left. Both of them stepped forward and grabbed Stella. Stella gasped.

"I don't leave nothing to chance," Boss said.

Henry was horrified. He couldn't let this bully take one of his friends. Henry flew forward with a determined look. "Leave her alone!"

Boss laughed. "Not a feather will be harmed as long as you get me my forty pounds of seed money by tomorrow morning. I want the mixed seeds and don't bring me the off-name brand; I want the good stuff. Meet me in this exact spot at eight o'clock and don't try anything stupid or your little finch here will be added to the deer meat!"

Stella looked at Henry with fear, her eyes pleading with him to come through. Henry started to fly toward Stella but Jay-Jay grabbed him and held him back.

Boss looked at Stella and asked, "Did you eat? I gots garlic seed. You're gonna love it. Let's go boys."

The Boss and his posse flew away, taking a wide-eyed Stella with them. Henry hated to watch Stella go looking so scared. On one wing, he hoped her southern sass would remain hidden. Boss didn't look the type to put up with that but, on the other wing, Henry knew her strong southern ways could help her get through it until he freed her.

Henry shook free of Jay-Jay's hold. "I cannot believe this! We have to save Stella."

"We have to find that seed money! Where is it, Vinnie?" Jay-Jay asked.

"I don't know."

"What?" Henry and Jay-Jay shouted in unison.

Victoria chimed in. "That's the Italian mob boss of New York! He migrates all over the world claiming he is owed seed money. My friend Ana Dora Elsa Inez Maria Rosa Silvia told me all about him. He did the same thing to her Papi and Mami and almost cost them their whole winter supply of seeds. He sells the seeds to the birds living in the zoos that can't get their beaks on those kinds of seeds. He makes a fortune."

"So we find as many seeds as we can and bring them to him and we are good, right? Stella will be released?" Henry asked.

"That's what he said," Vinnie replied with hope.

"Yeah, but where are we going to find forty pounds of seed and be able to carry it back in time?" Victoria asked.

Henry glanced around. He moved closer to the edge of the canyon. A good distance away he could see a shop and this gave him an idea. "What about the Grand Canyon gift shop? Do they sell birdseed?" Henry asked.

"How do we get in there and get a forty-pound bag of seed out without the humans seeing us?" Vinnie asked.

"It's going to take all four of us!" Henry said with conviction.

Fun Fact: When vultures locate a carcass by smell, sight, or the sound of other birds feeding, they approach it quickly before other predators find it.

CHAPTER THIRTEEN

Save Stella

A sign with the gift shop hours hung on the door. It read: "8 a.m. to 8 p.m." Henry, Jay-Jay, Vinnie, and Victoria looked at the large clock turning from 7:50 to 7:51 p.m.

Henry gulped and, if he was being honest with himself, he wasn't feeling confident about getting Stella back. However, as always, Hanna's words seemed to come to mind. Hope. It is hope. Henry smiled. "We don't have much time. We need to get in and get out fast!"

"But how?" Vinnie asked.

A family of four was at the checkout counter paying for their purchases before heading toward the door. Henry looked at them with a nod. This might be their only chance.

Suddenly his thoughts were interrupted by a loud "*Screech*!"

They all looked around, confused, until they looked up. In the sky they saw Slade. He had found them once again.

"Uh, amigos? We have company," Vinnie stated.

Henry looked back at the door. They needed to get in now! The family of four was heading out.

"Fly in as fast as you can! That door won't stay open long!" Henry prepared them.

The door swung open. They flew in, making it just in time as the door sealed tightly closed behind them. Slade flew into the glass and slid down the door. A huge bump formed on his head. Henry, Jay-Jay, Vinnie, and Victoria flew to the edge of a display where several pieces of jewelry hung. Jay-Jay picked up a shiny blue ring and slid it around his neck. Henry looked at him with a don't-play-around warning look.

"For Stella, as a 'good job, you survived the Italian mob boss vulture of New York' gift," Jay-Jay defended himself.

Henry rolled his eyes, "How about we find the seed and get out of here, and that way she can have the gift of life?"

"I mean, your idea is good too but it's just so shiny. I like shiny." Jay-Jay shrugged as Henry flew off. He left the ring around his neck and joined the others as they flew away from the stand and headed toward the very back of the store. A green sign read: "Birdseed" and an arrow pointed down.

"Of course it's in the very back of the store. Just our luck," Victoria complained.

They saw a stack of birdseed that read: "Off-brand birdseed is half price." They all scooted away from the off-brand birdseed, since Boss clearly specified his preference. They finally got to the high quality birdseed section, but the shelf was bare.

"Now we're in trouble," Jay-Jay groaned.

"We've been in trouble before!" Henry said. "And we found a way out. This is no different."

Henry hovered over the bags of seed and then discovered a top shelf with more seed. The sign read: "The best birdseed in the world!" Henry smiled. Hope. It was hope. Forty pounds of high quality birdseed, one bag left. He looked back at the clock – 7:55.

"Y'all, up here!" Henry called to them.

Jay-Jay, Vinnie, and Victoria flew up to meet Henry, who hovered over the large bag. They all landed on either side of it.

"This is it. We need to push it to the ground. The closer we fly to the ground the less likely we are to drop it and the less chance of being seen by the humans," Henry told them.

"Yes, I think it best the humans don't see a flying forty-pound bag of birdseed leaving the store without us paying for it," Victoria said.

Jay-Jay looked at her with a furrowed brow. "Right, and four birds trying to explain that we don't have the human money to pay for it would be an even bigger surprise."

Henry watched as the clock changed to 7:56. He was concerned. Could they really pull this off? "Okay y'all, we need to get out of here. We have exactly four minutes."

They all flew behind the seed bag and pushed with their wings. The bag moved half way. They pushed again, the bag dangled off the edge of the shelf. One more push and the bag fell to the floor with a loud thump. The human behind the cash register, a young college student dressed in full western attire, looked up. His nametag said George.

"What the heck?" George asked in his western drawl.

George walked toward the back of the store where Henry, Jay-Jay, Vinnie, and Victoria were using all the strength they had to fly the forty-pound bag of seed behind the end of an aisle. They made it behind the aisle just in the nick of time. George looked and saw nothing. Scratching his head in confusion, George looked up at the clock, which now read 7:57.

"Yee haw! Three minutes until closing time! Might have to close a minute early in celebration. No one's coming in anyhow," George said aloud.

Henry, Jay-Jay, Vinnie, and Victoria looked at each other in horror. They positioned themselves so that everyone had a side. Henry and Jay-Jay stood in the front and Vinnie and Victoria stood in the back. They flew low to the ground, straining as they made their way to the last aisle before the door.

"Move fast!" Henry said frantically.

They all flew as fast as they could until they were right in front of the door. The only problem was how could they get out of the store when the door was closed?

"I don't think we thought this through all the way," Jay-Jay said.

"The human is coming!" Victoria cried out.

George was heading their way. Henry smiled. He had an idea. Henry flew up in the air heading toward George. Jay-Jay, Vinnie, and Victoria gasped in shock. Henry circled around George's head and chirped a lovely tune.

George jumped back with surprise. "Whoa! Hey there little guy. Thought you were a butterfly at first. You stuck in here, huh? Follow me. I'll open the door; you fly out. You understand what I'm saying?" George asked.

Henry glanced down at Jay-Jay, Vinnie, and Victoria and nodded for them to move when the time came. They looked worried. Henry understood their worry—he had to keep George's attention so the three of them could get the bag out.

Vinnie flew to the middle of the bag and motioned for Victoria to lift the bag from the back. Jay-Jay saw the plan and positioned himself in the middle center of the bag. They lifted the bag with all their might and waited on weak, trembling legs.

"Okay little guy, head out now," George told Henry.

George opened the door and Henry hovered until he saw that they flew the bag outside. Only after the seed was outside did he fly out.

"Goodbye, little fella. It's time for George to head out," George said closing the door.

The clock on the wall changed from 7:59 to 8:00 and George turned the lights off. Henry hurried to the bag of seed where Jay-Jay, Vinnie, and Victoria were resting on top of it, clearly exhausted.

"Good job, Henry! Now if jou could only think of a way to get George to carry this heavy forty-pound bag of seed to the mob boss," Vinnie said.

"That would be marvelous," Victoria added.

Jay-Jay held his side, breathing heavy from exerting himself. "Very, very marvelous. My feathers should not be put through this stress. I have a certain look I'm going for . . . youthful."

"Don't forget about Stella; she also has a certain look she's going for . . . a stay- alive look! Now stop complaining and let's start moving this bag!" Henry yelled.

"*Screech!*" The four birds froze. Slade flew above them.

Vinnie looked up at Slade. "Not good Amigo."

"He's come back for revenge. We don't have time to hide," Henry said. "I have to fight."

"Are you loco? That eagle's going to eat and swallow jou in one bite," Vinnie told him.

"Henry beat him before, and with our help he can do it again," Jay-Jay said.

"What do jou suggest?" Victoria asked.

"He's after me. I'll do the distracting. You three start moving that seed!" Henry said with urgency.

"No way!" Jay-Jay said and shook his head. "I'm helping you."

Vinnie stepped forward too. "I got jour back, man."

Vinnie put his wings in fists and began boxing the air for practice. Slade flew straight toward them. There was no more time to discuss a plan. Henry flew to the left, Jay-Jay flew to the right, Vinnie kept boxing the air, and Victoria threw herself over the bag of seed. Slade headed full speed toward Henry!

"*Screech*!" Jay-Jay warned Henry.

Henry hovered until Slade was almost upon him, then he flew up and out of the way making it in the nick of time. Vinnie picked up a pinecone from the ground and threw it toward Slade, hitting him on the back. Vinnie smiled and flexed his bicep in triumph.

"That's right, you big bully! No one messes with Vinnie!"

Slade turned toward Vinnie in anger.

"Vinnie!" Victoria warned her brother, who was too busy flexing to notice Slade coming straight toward him.

Vinnie searched the ground for anything else to throw but couldn't find anything nearby.

"Hey ugly! Over here!" Jay-Jay yelled at Slade.

Slade turned and started toward Jay-Jay. Vinnie wiped his brow in relief. Jay-Jay flew as fast as he could, but Slade closed the gap between them. Slade reached his beak out and snapped at Jay-Jay, catching one blue tail feather in his beak.

Jay-Jay felt the pinch followed by a burning pain. "*Screech*!" Jay-Jay cried out.

Jay-Jay made a quick turn and glanced back at his tail feathers. Pure rage filled his body.

"No one messes with my tail feathers!" Jay-Jay charged after Slade who was heading for Henry.

"No Jay-Jay! I got this," Henry told his friend.

Henry hovered and flew left when Slade flew right, and right when he flew left. Henry had Slade going in circles until Slade was so dizzy he clumsily fell to the ground on top of the seed, nearly landing on Victoria.

"Jou loco? Your Papi and Mami don't teach jou no manners?" Victoria scolded Slade.

Victoria leaned back and came toward him with a huge punch, knocking him unconscious. Henry, Jay-Jay, and Vinnie joined her by the bag of seed. Jay-Jay gave Slade a kick in the tail feathers.

"Nice work everyone!" Henry smiled.

"That eagle ain't going to bother jou no more!" Victoria said proudly.

Henry glanced down at Slade and leaned closer. . Suddenly, out of nowhere, a falcon swooped down and lifted Slade, taking him with him with the help of the other falcons. Henry sighed. He was so close but there was no time to think about it. Henry looked skyward. The night was almost over. The crown of the sun was slowly coming up. They had to get the bag of seed to Boss or Stella would be a goner.

"We need to hurry!" Henry said.

Henry, Jay-Jay, Vinnie, and Victoria each took a side of the bag of seed and flew up and away.

Fun Fact: Vultures are recyclers as they are able to strip a carcass in just a few hours; they keep the environment clean and disease-free.

CHAPTER FOURTEEN

Shady Deals

The sun came up over the horizon. The four exhausted birds collapsed on top of the forty-pound bag of seed. Boss, his posse, and Stella approached the birds. Boss rubbed his wings together and smiled a wide, greedy smile.

Henry felt a surge of relief at seeing Stella again. She seemed concerned but it didn't look as though she had been harmed. They made eye contact and Stella gave Henry a small smile. He could tell she was also relieved to see they had found the seed.

"Well, well, well boys and girls, lookie what we got here. High-quality birdseed. So nice of you to bring it," Boss said.

Henry, Vinnie, and Victoria straightened up and stood to face Boss. Jay-Jay stayed down, still trying to catch his breath. Jay-Jay lifted one of his wings to show Boss he acknowledged him.

"No problem, Boss," Jay-Jay said breathlessly.

Boss saw Jay-Jay resting on his seed. "Get off my seed, Jay!" Boss shouted.

Jay-Jay scrambled off the seed. They all faced Boss. Jay-Jay lifted the ring off his neck and pointed to it, trying to show Stella her gift. Boss took the ring from Jay-Jay and placed it on his own neck.

"Nice touch," Boss said.

"That was actually for Stella," Jay-Jay informed him.

Henry elbowed Jay-Jay in the stomach to quiet him.

"Ouch!" Jay-Jay said. "Right, well it looks better on your neck anyway," Jay-Jay complimented Boss.

Boss looked at Stella. "I gotta say, I'm going to miss you, Sweet Tea. You've got sass and I like that. You still have that garlic bread Mamma packed you?"

Stella nodded. Henry looked between Boss and Stella in confusion.

"Anyway, we got your seed. Now release her," Henry said.

Boss turned to his posse and nodded. They pushed Stella forward.

Henry took a deep breath and remembered a saying his mama would always say, "How do you know if you don't ask?"

Henry spoke to Boss: "I have a request."

Boss looked at Henry. "You're requesting something from me?"

Henry gulped. "My sister has the bird disease. I know you travel all around the world. I thought you might have access to a special nectar I heard about. Could you tell me where to find it?"

Boss looked at Stella now. "Is this true, Sweet Tea?"

"It's the honest to goodness truth," Stella replied.

Boss's eyes softened. "My grandma had the bird disease. This nectar you talk about works. But it doesn't come free of charge."

"How much?" Henry asked.

"I only ask for Sweet Tea's wing in marriage," Boss said.

Stella's beak dropped open in astonishment but as soon as she recovered she replied, "You must be three gallons of crazy in a two-gallon bucket!"

Boss roared in laughter. "I knew I'd get one last southern quote from you Sweet Tea. I'm only kidding." Boss turned to Henry now. "I'll see what I can do. If I find it, I'll fly the nectar to you myself. No marriage proposal needed."

Boss nodded toward the bag of seed. His gang headed for the seed.

"Good luck lifting that, fellas. It's not easy!" Jay-Jay told them.

The four mob vultures easily lifted the bag of seed and flew off with Boss.

Jay-Jay shouted after them: "Right, well it gets heavy about halfway through your trip!"

Stella flew forward hugging Henry and Jay-Jay tightly. "Y'all, thank God you made it. The food was amazing but they wouldn't let me bathe. Anyway, he does have a strong love of family and that makes me think he will come through for you Henry."

"I'm so glad you're okay, Stella," Henry said holding her closer.

"Now what, Amigo?" Vinnie asked.

"Now we say our goodbyes," Henry said.

"We will miss jou guys." Victoria sniffed.

"Thank you Vinnie, Victoria. We won't forget you two." Henry wiped a tear.

"I wish jou guys a safe trip back home. Bring that sister of jours once she's better," Vinnie encouraged them.

"I will. Thank you for showing us the Grand Canyon," Henry said.

The goodbyes were bittersweet and Henry vowed to bring Hanna to the Grand Canyon one day.

***

Soon, Henry, Jay-Jay, and Stella flew over the welcome sign to New Mexico. They saw huge bright hot air balloons. There were so many different colors and designs. They smiled as they flew around the balloons.

A little blonde-haired girl in a red and white striped hot air balloon giggled in glee, "I love New Mexico's hot air balloon festival!" she said happily.

Jay-Jay nearly flew into one. Stella giggled.

"I wouldn't laugh Stella, you're about to fly into one yourself," Jay-Jay scolded her.

Stella made a large circle around a pink flowered hot air balloon. "I'm going around them Jay-Jay!" Stella showed off by doing circles.

"I can't wait to tell Hanna about this!" Henry said.

They landed on top of one of the balloons and let it take them for a ride. Henry grabbed his journal and drew one of the balloons.

"*Screech*!"

Henry, Jay-Jay, and Stella looked up to see Slade flying through the hot air balloons, looking for them. Henry threw his journal back into his backpack and dove down toward the ground with Jay-Jay and Stella behind him. They landed on the dirt ground where a large running bird nearly ran them over before he made a screeching halt. They had once again avoided Slade.

"Kindly get out of my way. You cost me a tasty mouse!" the large, gangly bird said tapping his foot.

Henry was intrigued. He had never seen such a bird as this one. "What kind of bird are you?" Henry asked.

"I'm a roadrunner. My name is Ron. Now, who's going to help me find that mouse?"

Stella asked, "Can't you fly to get the mouse?"

"I could, but I spend most of my time on the ground," Ron explained.

"Look at Ron's toes!" Jay-Jay pointed.

Ron's toes were very different. Henry couldn't stop looking.

"What about my toes? I have four toes on each foot. Two face forward and two face backwards. It helps me run as fast as I do," Ron told them.

"Awesome! You're what my mama would call unique. Which means different in a good way," Henry said.

Ron eyed Henry then looked at all three of them in irritation.

"You are what I would call a freak," Jay-Jay added his two cents.

Stella jabbed Jay-Jay in the ribs.

"Ouch! Why does everyone always hit me in the same spot?"

Stella bopped Jay-Jay on the head for good measure.

"Stop playing games and let's talk about my mouse," Ron said clearly annoyed.

"We would love to help you but we are on our way home to Louisiana," Henry told Ron.

Ron considered this and then smiled with a thought. "I also like small, tasty birds. I prefer mice but I will take what I can catch!" He eyed Henry and his stomach growled.

"Um . . . I think we can find the time to help our good friend Ron," Henry said.

Jay-Jay sucked in some air ready to screech but he didn't get the chance.

"*Screech!*" Slade beat him to it.

Several mice ran out from the tall grass. Ron noticed and took off full speed toward them.

"Okay who stole my thunder?" Jay-Jay asked.

All that was left of Ron was brown dust in the air stirred up from his departure. Slade continued to circle above them, searching.

"*Screech*!" Slade continued above.

Henry, Jay-Jay, and Stella backed up until they were hidden by the tall wheat stacks.

Fun Fact 1: Roadrunners can run up to 17 mph. Their entire body is designed for fast running as they have long legs and a long straight tail to help balance when running.

Fun Fact 2: Greater roadrunners are one of the few birds that have the ability to kill poisonous rattlesnakes. Even though these are solo birds, they will work together when they have to kill a snake. One roadrunner distracts the snake while the others target the snake's head with their sharp beak.

CHAPTER FIFTEEN

The Pet Collector

Henry, Jay-Jay, and Stella flew over another sign, one that read *Welcome to Texas!* They glanced down and saw a bunch of strange birds running frantically across a field. They took cover under a large oak tree and made gobbling noises.

The trio flew down together. Henry was determined to meet these interesting birds he was unfamiliar with. They landed on the ground among the nervous birds.

"I don't know what language they are speaking but here in Texas there is no telling. I read in my book that some of the humans here speak Spanish. Maybe their birds do too. I bet gobble gobble means hello in Spanish," Henry said.

Jay-Jay and Stella nodded in agreement. The strange birds looked at their bird visitors with great confusion and stopped gobbling. They looked back and forth at each other.

Henry stepped forward to speak. "Hello, my name is Henry Humming. Gobble!"

A pretty girl bird with a high pitched, stern voice stepped forward to ask: "Are you making fun of us, you mean little hummingbird?"

"Not at all! I'm trying to speak your language," Henry explained.

Henry, Jay-Jay, and Stella flew to a low branch so they could be out from underfoot of the birds, who seemed to be getting more anxious.

"What does 'gobble' mean?" Jay-Jay asked.

"That is our way of speaking to each other. It's our sound. Surely you three have a sound of your own," an older bird said.

"*Screech*! That's *my* sound," Jay-Jay told them.

The birds moved from side to side clearly annoyed by Jay-Jay.

"Please don't do that again! We are hiding and you may have blown our cover," one young bird said.

"Why are you hiding? What kind of birds are y'all?" Henry asked.

One of the larger ones stepped forward. He had a long wheat stem in the corner of his mouth and he was taller than the rest. He spoke to them with a heavy western accent, "Yer lookin' at wild turkey. The name's West. We are hidin' from the hunters."

"It's almost time for the humans' Thanksgiving feast. We ain't waitin' around these parts bein' that we are the number one target. We are tryin' to run and hide before we end up on the dinner plate," West explained.

Jay-Jay made a gagging sound with his beak in disgust.

"We are the largest North American game bird and unfortunately we taste mighty good. The humans don't like nuts, berries, and insects like us, eh?" West said.

"*Screech!*" Jay-Jay screeched as loud as he could.

West frowned, "Quit yer yammerin'! You'll send the hunters right to us if you don't stop!"

"Run! That is *my* sound. I make it to warn other birds of danger. Those hunters are coming this way now!" Jay-Jay warned.

The hunters emerged from the rows of corn and into the empty field. They were camouflaged and had hunting guns resting on their shoulders. The wild turkeys took off running in a cloud of dust, saying gobble gobble as they left. Henry, Jay-Jay, and Stella watched as all the wild turkeys dashed away.

"Nice meeting you!" West called over his shoulder.

The hunters ran after the turkeys. A little boy was running along the side of his father trying to keep up. He had a solid wood cage in one hand and bread crumbs in the other. On the cage there was an orange sheet of construction paper with the green painted words "Bart's bird." Henry, Jay-Jay, and Stella were so concerned with making sure the turkeys got away that they didn't see the young boy approaching them with a huge smile. Bart grabbed all three birds off the branch in one sweep of his arm and put them in his cage.

"What's happening?" Stella asked in fear.

"We have been caught!" Henry said.

Jay-Jay panicked. "Are we Thanksgiving dinner?"

"I think more like pets," Henry answered. "Again."

They bounced around in the wooden cage looking at each other in fear.

"We have to fly out as soon as he opens this cage. I'm nobody's pet!" Jay-Jay squawked. "Plus, I doubt this kid will give us a spa day!"

"Can anything else go wrong? Hanna is on borrowed time. Who knows if I can find the rest of the items for the cure? This is hopeless," Henry said sinking to the floorboards of the cage.

Jay-Jay and Stella tried to console him but Henry stayed planted to the floor. Stella kept a wing around him letting him know she was there for him.

Bart and his dad walked toward a red pickup truck. Bart held his wooden cage up proudly to show his dad.

"Dad! Dad! I have three new birds," Bart told him.

Bart's dad was too busy waving at another hunter and he didn't hear his son.

"We lost those turkeys but we will come back tomorrow," Bart's dad said.

They jumped in the truck and took off. An hour later, Henry slowly got to his feet, patting Stella in thanks. The trio saw a two-story red brick home come into view. They bounced and flopped around in the cage as Bart jumped out of the truck and ran up the pebbled walkway that led to the front door.

"Mom!" Bart screamed as he ran toward the kitchen. The savory smell of roast filled the air and the birds felt their own extreme pains of hunger fill their bellies.

Bart's mom came around the corner wearing a white and pink apron covered in hearts. She smiled when she saw her son and husband were home. She kissed Bart on the head and then her husband. Bart tugged on his mother's skirt.

"I made roast and potatoes," Mom said.

"Sounds great, honey. No luck with the turkeys today. It was like they knew we were coming," Dad said.

"Mom!" Bart tried to get her attention again.

"Not now, Bart, go upstairs and wash your hands before dinner," Mom told him.

Bart sighed, shrugged, and brought his cage to his bedroom. Henry, Jay-Jay, and Stella peeked out the hole. They saw a blue and white striped comforter covering Bart's twin bed. There was one large window above the bed overlooking a huge yard with a swing set. Bart placed the cage on his bed and ran out of the room.

"We need a plan," Henry said.

"No kidding. Does *The Seeds of Life* have any answers?" Jay-Jay asked.

"Y'all look!" Stella pointed through the hole in the cage. They all smashed together to peek out. They saw a dresser and some shelves above it. There was a fish tank on the dresser with fish in it, a clear glass box with a turtle in it, a large snake in a clear plastic container, a rabbit in a wire cage, and an ant farm. They looked away from the dresser to the shelf where there was a framed picture of Bart and four cats.

"What are the odds those cats are in this room, too?" Jay-Jay asked.

"I don't like them," Henry answered.

"*Bam*!"

"What was that?" Stella asked.

"Meow."

"Good odds," Jay-Jay said.

A large calico cat jumped on the birdcage. The other three cats circled the cage. They were pleased to find this new treasure.

Henry, Jay-Jay, and Stella backed up into the far corner of the cage.

Henry tried to reassure his friends and said, "We are perfectly fine. That hole is not even big enough for *me* to get out."

"Yes, but our way of escape is not looking good at all," Stella chimed in.

"Why aren't they going after the fish?" Jay-Jay questioned.

"Maybe they are tired of fish," Henry guessed.

Jay-Jay looked at Henry as though he had lost his mind. "Gee, that's the comforting news I was looking for, Henry."

Luckily, the door swung open and Bart walked into his bedroom. He ran toward the cats near the birdcage, swatting them away.

"Shoo, shoo. Sooka get down. Pirate! Sunny! Scout! All of you get down now!" Bart yelled.

The cats lazily took their time getting down, not fazed by Bart's efforts to move them. They walked toward the door with their heads held high and grins that seemed to say, "We will be back."

"Don't worry. They're harmless. I had them all declawed," Bart told Henry, Jay-Jay, and Stella.

Jay-Jay whispered to Henry and Stella, "Oh . . . well now I can sleep at night. Never mind about their sharp feline teeth!"

"Shhh," Henry warned him.

Bart moved the cage from the bed to the top shelf next to the picture frame and above the fish tank.

"Hmm, what should I name you three?" Bart pondered aloud.

"Perfect, just perfect." Jay-Jay rolled his eyes and threw his wings up in defeat.

"Well, I'm going to think about that. For now, I'll get y'all some food," Bart told them before leaving his bedroom.

Downstairs in the kitchen, Bart searched the pantry for something to feed his new pets. Mom turned around with a sigh.

"You'll spoil your dinner," Mom told him.

"Not for me, Mom, I have three new bird pets."

"More pets?"

"I know the rules, keep them in my room."

"What kind of birds?" Mom asked with her hands on her hips.

Bart was excited to show Mom. "Come see!"

She followed him up the stairs and into his bedroom. She peeked in the hole to see Henry, Jay-Jay, and Stella.

"A hummingbird! I do love hummingbirds," Mom exclaimed.

"I caught him all by myself!" Bart said proudly.

"You will need some nectar for the hummingbird. You have a blue jay and a finch as well. Get a salt stick and sunflower seeds and that should do just fine," Mom said as she moved away from the cage. "You can't keep them long, though. They belong in the wild."

"Finally, a human with brains," Jay-Jay whispered to Henry.

Bart stomped his foot. "I need them for my collection!"

"Ahh!" Mom screamed in fright and jumped back with a hand held to her heart. Her eyes were glued to the snake. "Bart Star! What did I tell you about that snake?"

"No snakes in the house."

"It had better be gone before breakfast tomorrow. Now come and eat dinner."

Mom walked out of the room. Bart shoved the snake under his bed and looked at Henry, Jay-Jay, and Stella one more time.

"You're my new pets. Once I get my hamster, my collection will be complete," Bart said. He smiled and walked out of the room.

"This doesn't look good!" Henry said as he flipped through *The Seeds of Life* looking for answers.

Fun Fact 1: A wild turkey's gobble can be heard up to one mile away and is a primary means for them to communicate to each other.

Fun Fact 2: More turkeys are consumed on Thanksgiving than on Easter and Christmas combined.

CHAPTER SIXTEEN

Keeping the Enemies Close

Henry, Jay-Jay, and Stella watched as the sun went down and the moon came up. Bart was sound asleep, snoring in his bed. Jay-Jay and Stella fell asleep so Henry read and thought about their predicament. Eventually, he fell asleep on top of the book. They woke up with a start when they heard Bart open the cage. He put nectar, a salt stick, and sunflower seeds in the cage before closing the door. They could hear the roar of the pickup truck from outside and the front door downstairs open.

"Bart, time to go turkey hunting!" Dad called from downstairs.

Bart ran out of his bedroom.

"Poor West and the rest of the turkeys! I do hope they don't get caught today," Stella worried.

"Poor us!" Jay-Jay said.

"*The Seeds of Life* doesn't have much on humans," Henry told them.

The pet rabbit laughed at Henry. "You birds better get comfortable. Bart never lets his pets go. His mama has been complaining about that snake for over a year now."

Jay-Jay flew to the hole and peered out toward the rabbit.

"How long have you been here?" Jay-Jay asked.

"Three years," the rabbit said.

Stella moaned and slumped down in distress. "We're never getting out of here. We will never get home, never taste the clean seed again, or feel the fresh water from the birdbath. Who knows how my parents are doing without me there to count calories for them."

"I can't think about it. My Mama, Papa, and Hanna must be so worried. If they're even alive," Henry added.

"I can't stay here as a pet. No way!" Jay-Jay complained.

"When you find a way out, let me know," Rabbit told them.

"We will help y'all escape when we find a way," Henry told them.

"Not everyone wants to escape. The fish and the four cats love being Bart's pets," Rabbit said.

"Really? The fish don't mind the cats?" Stella asked, surprised.

"The fish had to deal with the sharks in the ocean, so the cats are a welcome relief," Rabbit explained. "How do you plan to escape?"

"Not sure yet. The only pets free to move around in this house are those cats. Are you on speaking terms with them?" Henry asked.

Rabbit chuckled, "Are you kidding? They've tried to eat me on several occasions. Quite frankly, I deem them horrible roommates. That's why I never leave my cage. I'm not going anywhere with those cats looking for dinner every chance they get."

"Is anyone here safe from those cats?" Stella asked frantically.

"What about the turtle?" Henry asked.

The turtle slowly moved to the clear plastic window in his box. "Turtle soup!"

"The snake?" Jay-Jay asked.

The snake slithered forward to say, "Play toy . . . just as soon be eaten when they are done pawing at me."

Henry, Jay-Jay, and Stella sank against the back of the cage with a sigh, feeling defeated.

The door to Bart's bedroom opened and Mom came in humming a tune while she put Bart's laundry away. Two of the cats followed her in—Sooka, the orange cat with green eyes, and Scout, the white cat with blue eyes. Mom left the room but the cats stayed. They jumped on the bed, their tails swished back and forth; they licked their lips, and stared at the birdcage hungrily.

"He should have had their teeth pulled the same day as the declawing," Jay-Jay said nervously.

"Excuse me, but I think it's quite rude of y'all to want to eat us, or any of Bart's pets for that matter," Henry told them.

Jay-Jay flew on top of Henry, tackling him to the floor of the birdcage and covering his beak.

"Have you lost your feathers?" Jay-Jay whispered to Henry. Jay-Jay kept his wings covered over Henry's beak. Jay-Jay peered out of the birdcage and shouted to the cats: "He's only joking, he ate some bad seed earlier. You know, I believe I hear the sound of milk being poured," Jay-Jay said, hoping the cats would believe his lie and leave.

The cats grinned at each other and remained on the bed. Jay-Jay stayed on top of Henry. He looked through the hole and saw that they weren't going anywhere.

"Let go of Henry. He has a plan. You do have a plan, right?" Stella questioned.

Jay-Jay let go of an irritated Henry. Henry shook his feathers out and moved closer to Stella, motioning for Jay-Jay to join them.

"Of course I have a plan," Henry whispered. "I just don't know if it will work."

Jay-Jay and Stella stared at him wide-eyed, waiting for him to explain.

Meanwhile, Sooka looked at Scout and said, "I call dibs on the hummer. I love the hard-to-catch breeds. Although there is a sense of loss, knowing I didn't catch him off guard."

Scout purred happily. "Yes, a shame. I get the jay. Always had a thing for blue."

"Should we split the yellow finch or let Pirate and Sunny have her?" Sooka asked Scout.

Scout thought for a moment before answering. "Oh, I don't know. They didn't mind taking the last of the cat nip did they?"

Sooka replied, "Good point. I call heads."

"Tails is fine with me," Scout replied.

Back in the birdcage, Henry tried to get Jay-Jay and Stella on board with his master plan.

"Do you two trust me?" Henry asked.

"I do. I just hope this works," Stella said.

"Go for it. I'm willing to try anything to stop myself from being a pet. By the way . . . if we make it out alive I think it best that no one finds out about this. The jays have certain standards to live up to and—"

"Can we get to the point here?" Stella interrupted Jay-Jay.

"Small relapse," Jay-Jay admitted.

"Here it goes." Henry crossed his feathers for good luck before calling to the cats outside the cage. "If you cats enjoy the pampered inside life as a pet then I would think you wouldn't risk being put outside or perhaps sent to the pound?"

"Put outside?" Sooka laughed Henry's words off.

"Sent to the pound? What makes you think Bart would ever do that to us? He loves us!" Scout told Henry.

"It's not working!" Jay-Jay whispered in panic.

Henry kept talking, "Of course Bart loves you, but he loves us too. He loves Rabbit, Turtle, Fish, and even Snake."

Snake hissed in an offended way at Henry. Sooka and Scout thought about Henry's words. Their interest was held, for now.

"He loves us more, Hummer." Sooka replied.

"Oh dear, how little you know! Cats are superior to birds and everyone knows we are superior to dogs," Scout informed Henry.

Scout laughed at his own joke and Sooka joined him in laughter.

Henry kept trying. "Really? Well if cats are so superior to dogs then how come a dog would have been able to get us out of this cage? How come a dog would know that Bart would not want his other pets eaten or else it would get sent away?" Henry asked.

"Abort plan! Abort plan! We are nothing but feather dust now!" Jay-Jay panicked. Jay-Jay kissed each wing. "Goodbye beautiful blue feathers."

Sooka and Scout looked at each other with uncertainty.

"Cats have nine lives. Can you say the same of dogs?" Sooka questioned.

"I hope those nine lives are intact, because the outside world is tough on a cat . . . oh and don't even get me started on the pound." Henry continued to paint the scary picture.

Stella chimed in to help Henry. "Imagine the fleas! Nothing sanitary about that."

"Fleas!" Scout said in disgust. Scout looked at Sooka and whispered, "I can't be seen with those outside street cats. Do you realize they are not even declawed?"

"That's as uncivilized as it gets," Sooka replied.

They looked toward the birdcage. "We're listening, Hummer."

With a look of hope, Jay-Jay lifted his wings in joy. Henry smiled.

"Get us out of this cage and get us out of this house," Henry told Sooka and Scout.

"Don't you think if we knew how to get you out of that cage we would have already?" Sooka asked.

"And don't you dare suggest we summon a dog. Yuck!" Scout added.

"The drool would end my days on the carpet. I can't even say we would have dibs on the bed at that point. Would we even want the bed after the dog had its disgusting fur all—"

Henry interrupted, "No dogs, okay! I was thinking you could use your teeth to make the hole larger," Henry explained.

"Uh Henry," Jay-Jay said with great concern.

Scout turned his head up in stubborn pride. "You want me to risk chipping a tooth? I think not!"

"Why don't you simply wait until Bart opens the cage and fly out. I'll make sure the window is open and not our mouths," Sooka said with a grin.

"I like that idea. I still don't trust them enough to have their teeth gnawing on the very cage we are in," Stella said.

"Yes, and thank you, by the way, for giving them that idea," Jay-Jay added.

Henry looked offended, "I thought you two trusted me?"

Jay-Jay and Stella looked down sheepishly, then Jay-Jay looked up in determination.

"There's no guarantee he will open the cage," Jay-Jay told the cats.

"Or the window," Stella added helpfully.

Henry smiled, pleased that his friends trusted him.

"I'll worry about the window. You three figure out a way to get Bart to open the cage," Sooka told them.

Everyone stopped talking at once. Noises from downstairs could be heard. All the animals listened.

Fun Fact: Domestic house cats will hunt for sport, not just to get nutrients, and so they sometimes kill for fun when not hungry.

CHAPTER SEVENTEEN

Fly Out

Bart pushed his bedroom door open in a rush. Sooka and Scout jumped off the bed and meowed while circling Bart's ankles. Sooka jumped onto the windowsill and pawed at the glass pane all while meowing loudly.

"You want some fresh air Sooka?" Bart asked opening the window.

Sooka smiled with pride and whispered to Scout, "Cats are so much wiser than dogs. Humph!"

Bart walked over to the birdcage but just as he was about to peek in the hole, Mom called him downstairs. He ran out of the bedroom. Henry, Jay-Jay, and Stella sat up in defeat.

"We were so close," Henry said sadly. He flew to the hole and peered out toward the open window. Their freedom was so close he could taste it.

"Nice job Sooka! Rabbit, I'm going to figure out a way to save you too," Henry informed Rabbit.

"Save me? Are you kidding? I'm staying right here as Bart's pet. After hearing those horror stories of street cats with claws I figure I'm safer in here with these pampered pusses," Rabbit laughed.

"Who are you calling a puss?" Sooka asked with irritation.

Scout hissed toward Rabbit. Scout was about to swat at him when they all heard footsteps approaching. Everyone stopped to listen.

Bart came up the stairs toward his bedroom. "Okay Ma! I have to feed the birds first!" The door opened and Bart walked in. He walked over to the birdcage, peeked through the hole, and saw Henry, Jay-Jay, and Stella lying down. They appeared to be dead. Bart gasped in shock.

"They can't be dead! I fed them well. Are you guys sleeping?" Bart asked. Swinging the cage door open, Bart reached for Henry.

"Now!" Henry whispered to Jay-Jay and Stella.

Henry fluttered out of the cage and into Bart's face, causing him to back up with a shout. Jay-Jay and Stella flew out toward the open window. Henry followed behind them.

Bart ran toward the window, reaching out but missing Henry by an inch. "My collection!" Bart cried.

Sooka and Scout jumped to the windowsill and watched as Jay-Jay and Stella flew away. They turned to look at each other in confusion when they didn't see Henry. Bart sank down on his bed with a sigh. Sooka and Scout turned around to comfort him until he smiled.

"Thanks good ol' pals. I didn't want those birds anyhow. I still want a hamster though. Would you two like that?" Bart asked them.

Sooka and Scout smiled. Pirate and Sunny, the other two cats, strolled into the room and jumped onto the bed with Bart. They purred with content.

Bart gave them all one last pet and headed out of his bedroom.

"Hey!" Henry called from outside. Henry hovered above the windowsill. "Thank you, superior beings, you are far better than any old dog!"

Suddenly, Slade swooped in toward the window.

"Henry, watch out!" Jay-Jay and Stella screamed in unison.

But it was too late; Slade swooped down and knocked Henry back into Bart's bedroom. Henry landed on the blue and white striped comforter with a thump. The items for the cure spilled out from his backpack. He couldn't get up fast enough. Slade flew into the bedroom and landed on the bed with an evil grin.

Sooka and Scout stepped forward to protect Henry. Pirate and Sunny licked their lips while approaching Slade. An unfazed Slade kept his eyes on Henry.

Henry tried to fly forward but Sooka stopped him. "I have to get those items!" Henry said.

"You'll get killed trying. Let us take him down. You can always get more material things," Scout said.

"Not like these. Those are ingredients to cure my sister."

Sooka looked at Henry then back at the items that Slade was taking for himself. Sooka leaped toward Slade but Slade used his left wing to knock Sooka off the bed.

"Looks like I have the cure now, Hummer. You're about to meet your maker," Slade threatened Henry.

Scout pounced on Slade and knocked the items out of his right wing.

"Think again," Scout hissed.

Henry rushed to gather the items while Scout and Slade fought. Henry called out to Jay-Jay, "Jay-Jay catch!"

Just then, the door to Bart's bedroom swung open and Bart and his mom came in. Mom looked at Slade in awe.

"Bart, quick, grab your birdcage! That's a golden eagle!" Mom said with excitement.

Slade flew out of the window with an angry screech once he saw Bart and Mom. The screech was so loud that Bart and Mom ran out of the room covering their ears.

"Who gets the hummer?" Pirate asked.

"No one. He goes free," Sooka said.

Scout lifted Henry up with his paw. Henry fluttered out and hovered above the window.

"You saved my life. Thank you," Henry told the cats.

"Superior cats, that's just what we do," Sooka said with a grin.

Henry smiled and flew away to join Jay-Jay and Stella, and when he reached them, they all hugged.

Back inside Bart's bedroom, Pirate was trying to figure out why they let Henry go.

"Is someone going to explain why we let a perfectly good dinner go?" Pirate asked.

Fun Fact: Cats, both domestic and feral, are one of the most common predators of non-nested hummingbirds.

CHAPTER EIGHTEEN

More Than One

Henry, Jay-Jay, and Stella flew as fast and as far away as they could from Bart's home. They flew until they were back in the fields where they met the turkeys. Only then did they take a moment to rest on the branch of a lone tree among the wheat fields.

All of a sudden, they heard a rush of air followed by a cloud of dust. Henry coughed and blinked his eyes to see what they were up against now. When the dust cleared, Ron the roadrunner stood there looking at the trio with a grin.

"Fly on," Ron said lowering his back and offering a ride.

Henry hesitated and then asked, "Where are you taking us?"

"Wherever you like. I had the best meal the other day thanks to you three and I heard all about your journey and your sister's illness. I just thought, you know there's someone I'd like to give back to," Ron smiled.

"Freaky Ron has a heart after all," Jay-Jay joked.

Stella jabbed Jay-Jay in the ribs and flew onto Ron's back. Henry laughed and followed suit. Jay-Jay rubbed his ribs but also flew onto Ron's back.

"So where are we going?" Ron asked Henry.

Henry whispered in Ron's ear and he seemed leery but nevertheless he took off in Ron fashion, leaving a perfect cloud of dust. Henry and Stella held on for dear life to the back of Ron's feathers. Jay-Jay grabbed Henry around the waist and screeched.

After what seemed like the longest, bumpiest ride of their lives, Ron finally stopped late afternoon by a steep stretch of rocky cliffs.

"You sure this is where you wanted me to drop you off?" Ron questioned.

"Positive. Thanks Ron," Henry answered.

"No problem. Hey, thanks for calling me unique. Real self-esteem booster. Good luck with everything," Ron said.

The trio waved goodbye to Ron as he tiptoed a good distance before taking off full speed and disappearing in a cloud of dust. Henry, Jay-Jay, and Stella turned back around and faced the high rocky cliffs that surrounded them. They saw the edge of an eagle's large nest perched on the side of the cliff. Henry took a deep breath. Two more items. One, he hoped Boss would deliver, and the other, well, this was where he would find it. But would he actually get the chance to get it? Or would he die trying? Henry shook the negative thoughts away. He didn't come this far to give up now.

"I read in my book that eagles often live near cliffs. There were a few maps showing common locations and well, I put two and two together and this is where Slade lives," Henry said as calmly as he could.

"I can see that. Why are we at Slade's?" Jay-Jay asked.

"There are two things left to complete the cure: the special nectar and the feather of an eagle," Henry stated.

Jay-Jay's beak fell in shock. Stella looked down.

"This is the one I've been in a bundle of nerves about," Stella said.

"You knew about this, Stella?" Jay-Jay asked her.

Stella nodded.

Jay-Jay looked between Henry and Stella but then focused on Henry. "You can't be serious, Henry. All those times he was near, why not then?"

"Don't you think I tried? It was never the right time. I was trying to save my life, our lives, and protect the cure. I couldn't take him by surprise while fighting for these things."

Henry wondered if Jay-Jay and Stella thought he was crazy. If he had to do this alone, he would. But he sure would love to have them by his side. Henry flew along the cliff and looked for a way to get to the other side unseen. To his delight, he discovered a cave behind some overgrown vines.

"Over here! We can fly through this cave to the other side and surprise attack him from behind," Henry said.

Stella looked into the cave. She was hesitant. Henry could see all of her fears coming to the forefront. The walls of dirt, the confinement, the darkness, and of course what they all feared: the unknown. What or who was waiting for them on the other side?

"Any other options?" Stella asked.

Henry flew into the cave. He would lead them. If something happened, he would be in the front to protect them. He flew further in.

Jay-Jay followed Henry into the cave.

"I guess not. Please no spiders, please no spiders," Stella chanted as she flew in and caught up to Henry.

Inside the dark cave, Jay-Jay flew into the back of Henry. "Sorry, can't see the wing in front of my face," Jay-Jay said.

Suddenly, they heard a roaring sound. Something strange flew toward them and the closer they got, the more ear-piercing the roar.

"What's that?" Stella asked frantically.

Before Henry or Jay-Jay could respond, the creatures flew all around them. Some of the winged animals started to attack them.

"Bats!" Henry said pushing one off his back. Henry hovered to the left and then to the right. He avoided them as best as he could. He dove low to the cave ground and flew forward.

Two bats attacked Jay-Jay. "Move aside, you dirty cave dwellers," Jay-Jay said as he punched one of the bats in the face.

Stella tried to avoid being flown into. Finally, Jay-Jay and Stella were able to join Henry low to the ground and fly forward as the bats flew above them in a frenzy. Henry squinted to make sure he was seeing what he thought. Sure enough, he saw a light ahead.

"Look, we're almost there," Henry encouraged them.

The trio sped up and flew out of the cave. They struggled to adjust their eyes to the blinding, bright light. Henry looked around the blurry, sun-blinding space in front of them and saw several nests. He closed his eyes and opened them again, blinking several times.

The image was clear now. Henry, Jay-Jay, and Stella saw that they were surrounded by the sky-high rocky cliffs. On the cliffs, there were several eagle nests with eagles in them. The trio backed up until a big rock of the cave wall hid them from sight.

"I did *not* see that coming," Jay-Jay said.

"This was going to be hard enough dealing with one eagle, but twenty? Thirty?" Stella gulped.

Henry scanned each eagle in its nest and said, "We need a plan."

"We need a miracle," Stella said.

"We need to leave before we die!" Jay-Jay corrected them.

"I know it doesn't look good, but at least we have the element of surprise. These eagles don't know we're here. We can slowly fly up the cliff, keeping behind the curves and corners. I'll yank a feather from Slade and we fly down. He is closest to this cave and his back is to us," Henry explained.

Jay-Jay gave Henry a look. "I'm sorry, is that the plan or your idea of some sick twisted joke? Because all I'm hearing is fly up, pull eagle feather, and fly away from thirty angry eagles while contemplating our afterlife. We're going to die!"

"You have a better plan?" Henry questioned him.

The trio stood in silence.

Henry spoke first: "Only days ago I would have never asked for you two to help me. But now I know I can't do it all and it's okay to ask for help. So, I'm asking."

Jay-Jay and Stella exchanged glances and nodded. "We're in," they said in unison.

Henry smiled. He wished he could guarantee them this would work. He wished he had a way of doing it without putting them in danger. He whispered a quick prayer and flew up the cliff about ten feet or so and scooted behind a curve, hiding himself from eagle eyes. Stella followed.

Jay-Jay gulped. He said, "Hello death wish," as he flew to meet them.

Henry whispered, "I'm the one that will get the feather."

"I thought we would pull straws," Jay-Jay said trying to lighten the mood.

Stella rolled her eyes. "Hush."

Henry flew another ten feet. Jay-Jay and Stella followed. They continued to do this until they reached the top. Slade's back was to them and he slept. Henry pulled his backpack open and reached for one of Slade's tail feathers. Jay-Jay glanced behind them and saw that one of the other eagles had spotted them.

"Uh, Henry," Jay-Jay whispered.

Henry yanked Slade's tail feather. Slade flew up with an agonizing screech and all eagle eyes turned on them. Henry stuffed the feather into his backpack as fast as he could. He looked up and saw the attention of the other eagles on him.

"Fly!" Henry yelled.

Stella and Jay-Jay zoomed down the cliff as the eagles headed toward them. Slade focused on Henry who headed in the opposite direction.

Slade grinned, "You've had the upper wing all along, Hummer, but now you're in my stomping ground! You're as good as dead!"

Fun Fact: Golden eagles are found in mountainous areas, canyon lands, riverside cliffs and buffs, and anywhere the rugged terrain creates frequent updrafts.

CHAPTER NINETEEN

Fly Away

Henry turned back to see Slade closing the gap between them. Henry's eyes darted toward the cave where he saw Jay-Jay and Stella flying. His friends were going to be okay.

Henry dove down, forcing Slade to fly down after him. Henry turned upward before hitting the ground and Slade barely made it to a stop before falling on the ground. Henry knew if he used his special hummer moves, he had a chance of getting out of this alive. He was smaller but that could work to his advantage.

A furious Slade recovered and followed Henry toward the other side of the cliff. Henry saw the sun was shining on a small part of the cliff, making a mirror-like image. Henry flew toward the mirror-like image with determination. Just before flying into the image, Henry dove down and hovered to the side as Slade rammed into the image.

Small, imaginary eagles, like spinning stars, circled Slade's head. A large lump formed and he fell to the ground. Henry turned in time to see Jay-Jay and Stella enter the cave. The other eagles, realizing they weren't going to get Jay-Jay and Stella, turned their attention to their injured friend Slade.

Henry flew toward the cave to join his friends; it seemed he was in the clear. But, as the other eagles scrambled away, there was a trembling noise and large rocks began to fall from the cliff. One large stone caught Henry's tail feathers and pinned him to the ground.

Henry's backpack flew forward, the contents of the cure spilling on the ground. Henry strained to reach the items but it was no use. Jay-Jay and Stella, watching from the opening of the cave, looked in shock and fear. They wouldn't leave their friend; they flew toward Henry.

The other eagles saw how injured Slade was and became irate. They charged toward Henry. Jay-Jay, with the help of Stella, quickly gathered the items and put them back in the backpack. Henry saw the eagles and pointed to his backpack.

"Find the nectar and take the backpack and its contents to Hanna," Henry told them.

Jay-Jay looked at the backpack, still on the ground, and then back at Henry. Instead of taking the backpack and leaving as Henry asked, Jay-Jay tried to push the boulder off of Henry's tail feathers. Jay-Jay moaned and groaned, but the boulder wouldn't budge. Stella helped Jay-Jay but their efforts didn't pay off. Henry saw the eagles were almost upon them.

"Come here. Jay-Jay, Stella, take it and go! Leave me, or this will all be for nothing," Henry pleaded with them.

"I'm not leaving you!" Jay-Jay said.

Again, Jay-Jay tried to push the boulder off Henry. Stella picked the backpack up and slung it over her wing. She stayed and attempted to help Jay-Jay push the boulder off of Henry.

"Hanna will die!" Henry shouted.

Stella moved away from the boulder. Henry nodded at Stella in thanks.

"Go," Henry told them.

Jay-Jay turned as the eagles screeched toward them. He looked at Henry. "We will come back for you," Jay-Jay promised.

Henry tried to smile, grateful for his friends. He knew he wouldn't be alive by that time but he appreciated the sentiment.

"Find the mob boss, get the nectar, and then tell Hanna I went on the best adventure of my life. Tell my family that I love them," Henry told them.

Jay-Jay wiped away tears. Stella touched Henry's face lovingly. Henry struggled to keep tears from falling.

"Hey Stella. Boulders are about as useful as a roadmap with no street names. I always wanted to use that one; it's my favorite," Henry smiled.

Stella choked and brushed tears off her face. "So you do listen to some of my good ole advice."

Henry looked between the two of them. "I couldn't have done this without you two."

The flapping of several eagle wings brought their attention back. Jay-Jay and Stella turned to fly away, the eagles following right behind them. Henry saw his friends were in trouble.

"I'm the one you want, you nasty bullies. I beat Slade over and over again," Henry taunted them.

Some of the eagles turned to see Henry and they took the bait, nodding in agreement. They approached him with evil smiles and killer gleam in their eyes. The rest of the eagles followed Jay-Jay and Stella.

Jay-Jay and Stella reached the cave and flew in. The eagles stopped, not wanting to go into the dark cave. As Jay-Jay and Stella flew through the cave, the bats flew in a frenzy above them.

Stella punched a rather large bat that flew into her and she almost dropped the backpack. The two got to the other side of the cave and took some time to catch their breath.

Jay-Jay looked at Stella in awe. "Who are you, and what have you done with Stella?"

"Henry's death will not be in vain. Hanna will have this cure," Stella said.

Jay-Jay patted Stella on the back in comfort as tears streamed down her feathery face.

Jay-Jay encouraged her, saying, "Let's get that nectar and go home!"

Suddenly, Jay-Jay and Stella heard loud clanking noises. They looked up to see Emmett and six of his older retirees following him.

"No way! Emmett?" Jay-Jay questioned.

Emmett flew over and the retirees followed. Emmett pointed to a black crow with graying feathers that wore bifocals. "This here is old Batbird. That's what we call him anyway. Quite the bird boxer back in the day."

Emmett put his wing on an old light gray finch that used a tiny parachute to assist her when landing. "Sugarcane here uses this parachute for more than safe landings. She's ready for a fight."

An older red cardinal wheeled forward on his roller skates. He wore a floppy white knit hat on his head. He lifted the hat in salute revealing a bald spot before putting the hat back on his head. "Call me Wheels," he said. "I use these roller skates when I'm on the ground. Helps me get around faster. My wings are strong but my feet are not."

"Watch out the way," a grumpy cockatoo with a grim look on his face said stumbling forward. "Where's the battleground?"

"That's Cranky. He fought for our country. Good old bird there. He is ready to use his battle skills," Emmett told them.

A hunched-over robin that wore pants high up to his chest spoke next. "I'm Arch. . Don't let the hunch fool you."

Emmett laughed and then put his wing on the last of his group. "And last but not least, this here is Leather."

Leather was a lovebird and he wore a leather jacket. He smoothed back his bird mohawk of gray feathers.

Emmett stood before them proudly. "These old birds aren't what they used to be, but they still have some fight in them."

Stella lowered her shocked brows and frowned. "It's too late y'all."

Emmett shook his head. "No sweetheart, it's never too late. Where is he?"

Stella pointed to the cave. Emmett turned to his six old retirees and waved them toward the cave, "Let's do this!"

Batbird pushed his bifocals up the bridge of his nose, Sugarcane lifted her parachute in excitement and almost tumbled over, Wheels spun in a circle on his roller skates and became dizzy. Arch lifted his pants even higher, and Leather took a comb out of his leather jacket and styled his mohawk upright into a point.

"I'm not getting any younger," Cranky said.

Emmett led the way and they disappeared into the cave.

Jay-Jay looked at Stella, "Now that's something you don't see every day."

"Bless their sweet hearts; it's just too late. We need to find that nectar and get to Hanna!"

Fun Fact: A lovebird can be single. It can be happy being alone as long as it gets a lot of affection and attention from its owner.

CHAPTER TWENTY

All Together Now

The rocky cliffs seemed darker now that it was later in the day. The angry eagles surrounded and attacked Henry over and over again. Right before Henry passed out, he saw a blurry image above his head. The mob boss and gang flew above him.

Back at the cave, Vinnie and Victoria Vulture came flying out. Vinnie had a black eye where Stella had punched him, mistaking him for a large bat. Vinnie rubbed his eye and straightened his sombrero.

"That war has begun already," Vinnie said to his sister.

Victoria looked around until she saw Henry. The eagles surrounded him. Slade woke up and he limped over to join his fellow eagles.

"That's Henry!" Victoria cried.

Vinnie and Victoria flew over to Henry. Slade remained in place while the other eagles backed up and flew a few feet back as Boss and his gang landed.

"Boss, I think you will find it interesting to know that this hummer was trying to gather the ingredients to the cure and turn a profit," Slade told Boss.

Boss pointed to a lifeless Henry, "This hummer is looking for the cure for one reason and one reason only and that's to save his dying sister. If he dies, you die," Boss said.

Slade gulped. Boss looked at his gang and nodded toward Henry. With extreme ease, the gang moved the boulder off of Henry. Henry remained still and his eyes stayed closed. They all watched for any signs of movement.

By this time, Emmett and the old retirees flew over. Boss and his gang flew up and out of the way as Wheels crashed into the boulder with his roller skates but recovered. Emmett moved closer to Henry.

"Son. Oh no, son. This wasn't the way it was supposed to go. Who did this?" Emmett asked.

Boss looked at Emmett and the old retirees in confusion. "Who are you guys?"

"Friends of Henry," Emmett said.

Boss nodded, "The eagles and the falcons are behind this. Sorry for your loss. I truly am."

Emmett looked down at Henry's lifeless body and then at the eagles. Emmett nodded at his old retiree friends, then yelled: "Charge!"

Emmett and the retirees charged toward the eagles. Emmett flew in a zigzag pattern. Batbird squinted to see, Sugarcane put her parachute in the backpack and flew into the air, Wheels crashed into one of the eagles and sent him flying, Arch head butted an eagle and knocked him unconscious. Leather used his mohawk like a sword, cutting into a group of ten eagles and injuring them all, including another he pinned against a rock. Cranky whipped one of the eagles on the bottom with a switch.

Cranky scolded the eagle: "Back in my day, you would have gotten your . . . "

The eagle screamed out, "Aaa!"

Cranky continued, " . . . handed to you for this behavior."

"Are you kidding me with this?" The eagle asked.

To the eagle's surprise, Sugarcane landed on top of him with her parachute. She was able to land just right allowing herself freedom while he was trapped under the parachute. Wheels ran him over with his roller skates. The eagle laid on the ground in disbelief.

Cranky stood over him. "What's the matter? You've fallen and can't get up? Get a haircut, punk!"

Emmett jumped on one of the other eagles and yanked some feathers from his head. The retirees continued to fight the eagles. Boss and his gang exchanged glances of surprise.

"Who knew the old geezer's club had it in them?" Boss said in admiration. Boss reached into his stash and pulled out the special nectar. "Highest quality nectar around," he said and dropped some of the nectar into Henry's beak.

Vinnie and Victoria waited in nervous anticipation. Boss dropped his head in defeat. But, when all seemed lost, Henry twitched and slowly lifted his head.

"Now that's some good nectar," Henry said with a smile.

Vinnie held a wing to his heart, "Oh Amigo, jou gave me a scare."

Victoria helped Henry up.

"Good to have you back, Hummer," Boss said.

Henry wiped happy tears from his cheek. He was so touched that these birds cared enough to find him. "Thank you. Thank you all."

"Come now, Hummer. Let's not get emotional," Boss said flicking a lone tear off his cheek before anyone could notice.

"And stay gone!" Emmett shouted.

Henry looked around Vinnie, Victoria, and Boss and saw Emmett and his retirees cheering.

"Emmett?" Henry said in shock.

Emmett turned around to see that Henry was alive. He flew over along with his retirees. "Son, you made it after all!"

"So did you," Henry smiled.

"This old hummer isn't what he used to be but he still keeps his word," Emmett said.

"Thank you, Emmett," Henry said.

Boss pulled out the vile of nectar. "You will need this to complete the cure," he said to Henry. "Now go find your friends, and go home to that sister of yours."

Henry grinned. Vinnie handed Henry a small note and said, "I forgot to give this to jou. My mailing address. Jou will write me on jour sister's progress right, Amigo?"

"Of course. Vinnie, Victoria, thank you. You didn't have to—"

Victoria stopped him, saying, "Jou loco? Of course we did. That's what friends do."

"Speaking of friends, I have two that believe I'm feather dust," Henry said.

They all nodded, embraced in a hug and watched as Henry flew off. While Emmett and his retirees scared all of the other eagles away, Slade remained. Malcom and the falcons landed before Slade.

"Where's the cure, Slade?" Malcom demanded.

"It's gone, as is the hummer," Slade said.

"How does a tiny hummer outsmart you and your pack of eagles?" Malcom questioned.

"He had the mob boss on his side," Slade said, pointing behind him.

Malcom tilted his head to the side and looked surprised, saying, "The mob boss!"

Vinnie nodded, "That's right, Amigo."

"You work for me now Slade. Your every move will be monitored and if you step out of line . . . " Mob Boss's crew stepped forward with their sharpened sticks. Boss motioned with the tip of his feather across his throat to show Slade what would happen.

Slade's eyes bulged. Boss's sidekicks surrounded Slade. Boss nodded and they all flew up and away. Malcom and the falcons watched as Slade was taken prisoner. They looked back at Vinnie and Victoria.

"And if jou know what's good for jou, jou will head back to jour falcon nest and stay there. The Boss has put an alert out for anyone that interferes with our friend, Henry Humming!" Vinnie said.

"It was all Slade's idea. I never want to see that hummer again," Malcom said in a shaken voice. With that said, Malcom and his falcons flew off.

"Jou sure know how to clear a room, Amigo," Victoria said with a laugh.

Fun Fact: When comparing eagles and falcons, it's interesting to know that eagles are very aggressive whereas falcons are not. Falcons surprisingly have pleasant character traits.

CHAPTER TWENTY-ONE

Home Sweet Home

Henry flew as fast as he could through the mossy trees until he saw Jay-Jay and Stella. He called out in excitement to them: "Jay-Jay! Stella!"

Jay-Jay and Stella turned in disbelief. They focused on the small blurry image that was Henry until he was close enough to make out.

Jay-Jay's beak dropped open in shock.

Stella cried out, "Well butter my butt and call me a biscuit; it's Henry!"

Jay-Jay tried to focus again, still in disbelief. "It can't be."

Henry flew into their open wings, nearly knocking them over. They hugged and cried.

"How did you do it, Henry?" Jay-Jay asked.

"Some of our friends we met along the way helped me out. Emmett, Vinnie, Victoria, and Boss," Henry told them.

Stella smiled and said, "Thank God."

Henry pulled back from them and held the nectar up for them to see. Jay-Jay patted him on the back in congratulations. Stella wiped a tear of joy.

"Let's go home," Henry said.

The trio flew and flew until the humid air seemed to suck their energy out. They stopped in a cypress swamp to rest a bit and eat. Henry looked around at the cypress trees, the moss, and the swampy waters. He took in the smell of rich soil and a mixture of salt and sweat. Henry's eyes widened; he had a gut feeling they were close to home.

They ate on a large oak tree with moss dangling from every branch. Henry spotted a trumpet vine while Stella licked from her salt stick she had taken with her from Bart's. Jay-Jay looked through Henry's backpack until he found some sunflower seeds and popped them into his beak.

"Oh my goodness," Jay-Jay said in shock.

Henry and Stella jumped up; they looked around for trouble.

"What?" Henry asked in a panic.

"Another eagle?" Stella asked.

"Another Bart?" Henry asked.

"No silly . . . a bright red shiny thing . . . down there," Jay-Jay pointed to a red wagon that was abandoned on the edge of the swampy waters.

Stella shook her head, and Henry opened up *The Seeds of Life*.

"*Screech*!" said Jay-Jay.

Henry dropped his book but Stella caught it before it fell into the water. Henry put the book in his backpack but not before giving Jay-Jay a look of irritation for letting out the loud screech that startled him.

"Now what?" Stella asked with irritation.

"Shhh!" Jay-Jay said.

Jay-Jay pointed with his blue wing. They looked down and saw a great snowy white bird with yellow toes.

"What kind of bird is that?" Henry asked. "And why is he wearing human stuff?"

Henry began to open his backpack and take out his book. He didn't want to take any chances with scary large birds after getting this far and securing the cure.

"Why don't you come ask me yourself? Choot!" the large white bird said.

Henry, Jay-Jay, and Stella looked back down to see the white bird smiling up at them. Henry nodded and they flew down, landing on a tall, thick green leaf. The large bird grinned.

"Well, how are y'all doing? I hope y'all are not trying to take these crawfish from me. I've been standing out here all day in this Louisiana heat waiting and I'm ready to eat!" he said.

"*Louisiana*!?" Henry, Jay-Jay, and Stella shouted in excitement.

"Louisiana. You know, the state that has a brown pelican as the state bird when everybody knows it should be the crawfish representing for 'em?" he informed them.

"How wonderful!" Stella exclaimed.

The white bird looked confused.

"My name is Henry Humming and this here is Jay-Jay and Stella Finch. This is actually our home state; we finally made it back. We have been traveling for so long," Henry said.

"I'm Sam and let me be the first to say, welcome home. Why would you ever leave this wonderful place?" Sam asked.

"We didn't have a choice. The hurricane took us to California," Stella explained.

"Ah that hurricane was rough on these swampy marshes, but the crawfish are back now," Sam said.

"What's a crawfish and what kind of bird are you anyway?" Henry asked Sam.

"You said you're from Louisiana, huh?" Sam asked.

"We'd never migrated or traveled until the hurricane. We lived in the same backyard year round," Jay-Jay said.

"Ah, well I'm a snowy egret and . . . wait, you never migrated before?" Sam asked, shocked.

"Nope. I'm a blue jay," Jay-Jay said proudly.

"I know birds, no need to give your breed." Sam stared at them but then answered Henry. "A crawfish is a tasty treat that lives in the swamps mostly. I would say they taste a little like fish but better."

Henry looked at Sam with more interest. "How tall are you? Why are you wearing yellow rain boots from the humans? Are you a pet?"

Sam tilted his head to the right and then to the left. His eyes never left Henry's. "You should get out more, Henry. I stand two feet tall and those are not human boots, those are my yellow toes. So you three have *never* migrated? I'd never know," Sam said, teasingly.

"Nope. The hurricane that took us to California was our first time seeing the world and learning about other birds. We have been trying to return home to our families ever since. How far is the town of LaPlace from here?" Henry asked.

"Not far at all; I'd say thirty minutes of fly time," Sam told them.

Tears welled up in Henry's, Jay-Jay's, and Stella's eyes.

"Thirty minutes?" they asked to make sure they heard him right.

"Miss home, do ya?" Sam asked.

"We are very ready to see our families. We don't even know how they made out after the hurricane," Henry told Sam.

"Before you go, who wants to try a crawfish?" Sam asked with a grin.

"Does it taste sweet?" Jay-Jay asked.

"Not at all."

"Then no way!" Jay-Jay replied, shaking his head.

"Is it salty?" Stella asked.

"Very salty!"

"I'll try," Stella said.

Jay-Jay stared at Stella in shock. "You do realize that crawfish comes out of these waters. The very water you see with the green muck and other birds in it? The water right here, the water you can't see the bottom of?"

"I know, but I figure I made it this long without a clean bath, clean seed, and my own nice and neat nest that I might as well go all out. So . . . hit me up, Sam," Stella said.

"Oh no, honey, I don't believe in violence."

Henry smiled at Stella; he was proud of her for trying new things. "She meant give her a crawfish, Sam, and while you're at it, I'll try one too. If Stella can do it, so can I," Henry said.

Henry and Stella tasted the crawfish. Stella smiled, for it was very salty, the way she liked her food. Henry, however, had a different tasting experience. He made a face of disgust. Jay-Jay laughed so hard he nearly fell into the swampy waters.

"At least I tried it," Henry told Jay-Jay. "Well, Sam, we have to be on our way. Nice meeting you," Henry said.

Sam nodded, a bunch of swamp water and moss hanging from his mouth. He watched the trio leave the swamp and fly over the mossy trees until they were mere specs.

A small fishing boat was speeding down the bayou. Henry and Stella flew low through the trees.

Jay-Jay flew ahead and yelled, "Race y'all home?"

Henry and Stella smiled, but their smiles faded and were replaced by looks of horror. Jay-Jay frowned in confusion.

"Jay-Jay!" Henry and Stella screamed in unison.

Jay-Jay turned back but it was too late; he was going too fast. He flew straight into the glass windshield of the boat. His body slid down the glass and fell into the swampy waters below.

Henry and Stella dove as fast as they could. The boat didn't stop and was already out of sight. Stella landed on a loose log in the water, looking down for any sign of Jay-Jay. Henry hovered over the surface. They saw a bright blue-feathered body pop up and out of the water. Henry flew over with fear and Stella helped him pull Jay-Jay out of the water. They brought Jay-Jay to a nearby tree stump. Henry turned Jay-Jay face up with his wing.

Stella looked down at Jay-Jay and then back at Henry. "Is he . . . ?"

"I don't know," Henry said worried.

Henry started to push on Jay-Jay's stomach and breathed into his beak. Stella cried.

"Come on Jay, you're stronger than this! You're a jay, remember? Jays can beat anything!" Henry encouraged his friend.

"Tell him he's handsome. He likes that," Stella said between sobs.

"Jay, come on friend, you're too handsome to have your life cut short like this," Henry said, trying anything to help.

Henry pushed on Jay-Jay's stomach again and again. Stella pushed Henry aside and breathed into Jay-Jay's beak.

They both froze when his wing lifted very slightly off the tree stump. Henry stared at Jay-Jay's wing in anticipation. Stella held her breath. Jay-Jay's wing twitched again. They looked at Jay-Jay's face and saw a huge grin. Jay-Jay opened one eye and then the next.

"I'm in my prime! No way I'm going out like that!" Jay-Jay said proudly.

Henry and Stella laughed out loud and hugged Jay-Jay so tight that water came out of his beak.

"Oh that feels much better. Okay, okay watch the feathers. I love y'all too." Jay-Jay laughed.

Jay-Jay stood up, rubbed his forehead, and felt a large bump. He shrugged and shook off the swamp water.

"How do I look?" Jay-Jay asked.

"Handsome as always," Stella replied.

"I'm going for confident these days," Jay-Jay said with a wink.

Henry smiled.

"Shall we try this again?" Stella asked. "Maybe this time we don't race?"

They all laughed and took off in the air, heading back toward home again.

Soon, they saw the familiar brick house with the large wooden porch. Henry, Jay-Jay, and Stella stopped on the porch swing. Henry took it all in. He wanted a minute to really realize that he went on an adventure and brought back the cure for Hanna. Stella was thinking how far she had come with her OCD tendencies and Jay-Jay realized looks weren't nearly as important as lifelong friendships. They all smiled at each other and took each other's wings.

"We started this together; we end this together," Henry proclaimed.

They flew together over the roof and landed on the bird feeder, which swung back and forth. As they looked around, they saw that the backyard looked exactly like they remembered—it had been restored after the storm. Henry stared at his wooden birdhouse and noted that the hole where his room was torn off by the hurricane had been fixed.

Stella looked into the birdbath and saw her dirty reflection, but turned away and looked toward her family nest. She smiled.

"Our families made it. I must go to my mom and dad," Stella said happily.

Jay-Jay looked at the birdbath and then back at Stella. "Aren't you going to wash off first? All you talked about the whole way home was having a cool bath," Jay-Jay reminded her.

Stella glanced at the birdbath and then back toward her nest. "I can do that later."

Henry swallowed past a large lump forming in his throat, "Well, I . . . "

Jay-Jay and Stella spoke in unison, "Go on Henry. Go to her."

Henry embraced them in a quick hug and flew toward his birdhouse. Jay-Jay and Stella exchanged glances.

"Wait!" Jay-Jay said as they flew after Henry.

Henry turned: "Your family?"

"Is right here; a part of it," Jay-Jay said.

"We didn't come this far to not see Hanna healed," Stella added.

Henry choked up with emotion and flew into his birdhouse with Jay-Jay and Stella following.

Henry stopped in his tracks and sucked in a deep breath of air. A featherless Hanna lay on a bed of pine needles in the living room. She turned her head weakly and saw Henry. Her eyes filled with tears. Henry let out the breath of air he had been holding and cried. He flew to his sister.

"You're still alive. Thank God," Henry said and hugged Hanna.

Hanna spoke softly, "I knew I'd see you again."

Papa Humming and Mama Humming came out from the back of the birdhouse and into the living room. They gasped in surprise and joy at seeing Henry.

"Henry! Oh God, how we worried and prayed for you to return to us," Mama flew to him and embraced him in a big hug.

Mama moved aside so Papa could hug Henry.

"I'm fine Papa. I'm here," Henry reassured him.

"We all are," Jay-Jay said.

Everyone smiled.

"Hanna, I have the cure," Henry told her.

Hanna spoke in a weak whisper, "I knew you could do it. But more importantly, did you have an adventure?"

Henry smiled, "Yes. I had an adventure, Hanna."

Henry pulled the tube of nectar from his backpack, grabbed a bowl, and put everything for the cure together into the bowl along with the nectar.

"Eat this," Henry offered it to Hanna.

Hanna tried to sit up but she was too weak. Hanna's eyes closed shut. Henry looked down at the cure and pecked it with his beak until it was in a liquid form. He poured the liquid down Hanna's beak and waited.

Everyone stood around her and prayed softly for the cure to work.

"Hanna? Hanna answer me. How do you feel?" Henry asked.

Hanna's body twitched but then fell still again. Henry looked down in distress. "What's happening? It should have worked."

Papa and Mama moved closer to Henry. Mama placed her wing under Hanna's nose. She looked up with tears in her eyes. Jay-Jay and Stella exchanged despairing looks.

"Henry, she's gone. She held on as long as she could. She waited for you," Mama said.

Henry's eyes welled up with tears. He couldn't believe it. He had worked so hard to get the cure, to fight battles, find his way back home to her and it was all for nothing. It couldn't end this way. Henry tried again. "Hanna! Wake up!"

Henry looked in the bowl and saw one last drop. He picked the drop up with his wing tip and carefully placed it in Hanna's beak. How could this be the end for his sister? She didn't deserve to go without a chance to fly and see the world. She was the reason he went on his first adventure. She was the reason he faced enemies and made allies. She was the reason he had hope. Henry felt an empty hole grow and spread throughout his body. He knew without Hanna he would never be the same.

Papa put his wing on Henry. "At least she saw you one last time."

Before Henry could respond, Hanna's body started shimmering and a warm glow surrounded her. A light shined all around them, and Hanna began to heal. Her feathers grew back, and she became stronger. Hanna slowly opened her eyes.

"Henry, you did it," she said.

In that moment, Henry felt the hole disappear and waves of relief flooded through his body. Henry hugged her tight. "Hanna, thank goodness. It worked! It really worked!"

Papa and Mama embraced Henry and Hanna all at once. Jay-Jay and Stella joined them. Everyone cried tears of joy.

Papa spoke first: "I'm proud of you Henry."

"Me too," Hanna smiled.

"We all are," Mama said and Jay-Jay and Stella nodded.

"Thank you for giving me a reason to see the world and find hope, Hanna. And I couldn't have done this without Jay-Jay, Stella, and some other special friends I met along the way," Henry said.

A few hours later, Henry had his journal open on the table. Hanna, Papa, Mama, Jay-Jay and his parents, and Stella and her parents were all gathered around the table. Henry, Jay-Jay, and Stella took turns telling of the great adventure they went on, of all the places they went, the birds they met, the cats, the humans, and the great battle against Slade. As Henry listened to Jay-Jay telling his triumphant moment of using the prickles to defeat Slade, he knew it was a blessed day. He knew many more blessed days would follow and he intended to make every day count.

Fun Fact: Female and male snowy egrets take turns incubating their eggs. As one mate takes over for the other, it sometimes presents a stick, almost as if passing a baton.

CHAPTER TWENTY-TWO

One Year Later

A year later brought another humid Louisiana summer to the backyard of 11 Holly Drive. Bees buzzed, trumpet vines spread over the playhouse, fresh, salty seed spilled over the feeders. Cool, clear water rippled in the birdbath and the whole backyard was bustling with birds. Henry had worked day and night with the help of Hanna, Jay-Jay, and Stella to put together a bird health fair. It was the perfect time, as Mr. and Mrs. Whitman had gone on their annual beach trip to the Mississippi coast.

Henry flew out of the birdhouse and admired their handy work. A handmade sign read: Bird Backyard Health Fair. The bird community all came out and even some neighboring yards of birds flew over to see what it was all about. Henry flew back to the birdhouse to get Hanna.

Jay-Jay, who was wearing a small cap, flew over to where Owen Owl and Doctor Redbird stood behind a booth. Jay-Jay took a vile of liquid and held it up.

"So this is all natural?" Jay-Jay asked.

Owen Owl answered, "Yes. Now if you use it for a week and still don't find your feathers coming back faster and thicker, you should see Doctor Redbird here."

Stella flew and joined Jay-Jay. She lifted his cap revealing a small bald spot on the top of Jay-Jay's head. Jay-Jay snatched the cap back and placed it on his head.

"Don't mean to ruffle your feathers, I'm just looking for something to tease you with later on when those fine feathers grow back, and along with it, your extreme vanity," Stella teased Jay-Jay.

"Ha ha, very funny," Jay-Jay grumbled.

Owen Owl chuckled. "No need to be startled. The temporary balding on Jay-Jay's head is seasonal molting. It's all a natural part of the molt cycle that all jays go through."

"Well, I'll take anything to speed this along and hopefully this is a one-time deal," Jay-Jay said taking the vile of liquid.

Stella was the first one to see Henry fly out of his birdhouse, followed by Hanna who quickly flew passed her brother with beautiful speed. Hanna landed on the bird feeder and Henry landed next to her a few seconds later. Stella and Jay-Jay flew to join them.

"Look at you, Hanna! One wing and you can still outfly Henry," Stella beamed.

"Must be the flying lessons Henry gave me," Hanna said with a smile.

"She's a natural. It looks like our health fair is a hit," Henry said.

"Everyone is mingling and learning all about the importance of natural healing as well as scientific healing. We will have the healthiest bird community around," Stella said.

"This was a great idea," Jay-Jay complimented.

Suddenly, a swoosh of black flew by and crashed into the birdbath with a splash. Henry flew over and helped Emmett get to his feet.

"Thank you, son. These old wings aren't what they used to be," Emmett said.

Emmett was visiting just like he promised and he was even considering retiring in their very backyard.

Hanna hovered over Emmett with a giggle.

"Look at you, sweetheart. Flying better than old Emmett here."

"Do you think this is a good place to retire, Emmett?" Henry asked.

Emmett leaned closer to Henry and asked, "What's that, son? You have to speak louder. Old Emmett's ears aren't what they used to be."

Doctor Redbird called out to Emmett: "I may have something that will help with your hearing."

Emmett flew over toward Doctor Redbird. Henry smiled. It was good to see his old friend here in Louisiana.

"Want to show them what you got, Hanna? A little entertainment, hummer style," Henry asked his sister.

Hanna nodded with excitement. Bob and Bonnie Humming came out of the birdhouse in time to catch her flight show. Hanna took off into the air creating the humming sound with her fast-beating wing. It was softer than other hummers as she only had one wing but it drew every bird's attention just the same.

Henry loved that Hanna had that unique quality that was so her; soft but strong, sweet but tough. Hanna flew higher before diving down and back up. She hovered a moment and then flew backward without a hitch. Henry never grew tired of seeing his sister fly.

It had been a happy year for the Humming family and Henry knew they had many more to come. Most would take place in this very backyard but some would come from their travels. Hanna did a perfect flip and joined her brother, Stella, and Jay-Jay back at the feeder.

The bird community clapped and cheered for Hanna. Henry and Hanna saw their parents clapping and cheering the loudest.

"That was fantastic Hanna," Henry said.

"Sweetie, that was flawless," Stella complimented.

"Sure was," Jay-Jay agreed.

Hanna beamed.

"So, I was thinking we should all go on an adventure. This time with Hanna," Henry said.

"Where y'all thinking?" Stella asked.

Jay-Jay spoke, "What about the east coast?"

Henry looked at Hanna and asked, "What do you say, Hanna?"

"I'll pack the nectar," Hanna said and smiled with excitement.

"This time I'll be prepared. Grooming tools, human repellent, tweezers for prickle removal, birdcage locksmith tools, and defense moves against eagles," Jay-Jay said lifting his wings and punching the air as his feet moved side to side like a boxer.

"Here we go again," Henry said and laughed.

Everyone joined in laughter. Henry was excited to embark on a new adventure with his sister and two best friends. Of course, he would always have a soft spot for the very first adventure where he learned to trust others, take risks, live for the moment, and most importantly, where he learned to always have HOPE.

THE HAPPY END.

Henry Humming® – Henry Saves Hanna

Dedicated to my wonderful daughters

Eliza and Madelyn

Henry Humming®  *Henry Saves Hanna*

More Fun Facts:

- Hummingbirds have tiny hairs on the tip of the tongue to help lap up nectar.
- A ruby-throated hummingbird flies 500 miles nonstop across the Gulf of Mexico during both its spring and fall migrations.
- A hummingbird's body temperature runs higher than a human's. A hummingbird has a normal body temperature of 105 to 108 degrees.
- Blue jays in extreme northern populations may migrate but most birds remain in the same areas year-round.
- Blue jays are highly adaptable to different habitats and can be found in different types of forests as well as cities, parks and suburban areas where trees are present.
- American goldfinch birds primarily eat seeds of plants including but not limited to thistle, ragweed, dandelion, and sunflower.
- American goldfinch can be found at feeders any time of year, but most abundantly during winter.
- The goldfinch's main natural habitats are weedy fields, floodplains, roadsides, orchards, and backyards.
- The golden eagle has been known to attack full-grown deer. They also eat rabbits, marmots, ground squirrels, reptiles, birds, fish, and large insects.
- Golden eagle pairs maintain territories that may be as large as 60 square miles and keep their nest in high places including cliffs, trees, or human structures such as telephone poles.
- Female golden eagles lay from one to four eggs.